Angels & Hunters

I0619481

Angels & Hunters: Book Two of The Dark Angel Wars

2017 © K.L. Stewart

Cover art 2017 © K. L. Stewart

All Rights Reserved.

ISBN: 978-1-938743-12-2

I. Klarissa's Vision

Wind howled through the black, twisted branches of the massive kial thieren trees and darkness covered the land far into the morning. A coldness beyond the natural workings of winter now seeped its way through the land. The scithronians, a small band of young thieves, had gathered when their seer had summoned them. They sat in the main hall of their den. Torches burned brightly in the sconces on the stoned walls which were built underground between the enormous roots of the kial thieren trees. Flames illuminated hundreds of eyes that glared from beneath hoods, garments, and furs, and lit up tips of weapons left out, only hinting at the many more that were too well hidden for the light to find. The gathering of rogues sat looking toward one young woman, the seer Klarissa. She stood before them, her vibrant, red hair blazed in the firelight, peeking from the edges of her black hood. Her eyes stared at them blank and white. The room of youthful orphans stared back, waiting anxiously for what she would say; waiting for the news of what she had seen afar.

She stared back, aware of them but only seeing the visions that came to her, patiently deciding what she would say to them. She saw things that she did not understand. There were creatures. They were like nothing she had ever seen before. Large and lethal, their limbs were weapons, and their faces contorted between human and demon. Silvery-black mingled with flesh and blood. They came from the barren lands, casting shadows wherever they trod. They came hungry for blood, with intent to slaughter. When she felt the time was right, she spoke.

"Creatures trample the land…made both of unnatural shadow and man. They must be stopped," she said. "Their intent is to aid the Shadow. To kill. They care not for riches. They have no value of life. They mean to convert us, or slaughter us." She saw also a council of gods. Some she knew the names of, others she had never heard of. "The order of the new world has not yet been decided. Angels, demons, and man all have a claim upon the land, upon the souls who thrive here. I cannot see who will be the ultimate victor, but it must not be the demons!

We must aid those who will protect us." She paused, and stared to the Southeast. "The angels, our protectors…they need us now. Time is against them but we will aid them." She reached out into the crowd, stretching her hand to one who sat near her. The young girl had a matted mass of black hair sticking out from beneath her hood. She was easily recognized as the thief Valassa. Klarissa pulled her close and whispered into her ear. The young thief's expression quickly changed from calculating to elation. Valassa was more than honored to be entrusted with the task that the seer now whispered to her. She nodded her head and patted the seer on the shoulder.

"I will do the honor!" she proudly agreed. Then she stepped away and immediately started seeking out and whispering to those who would help her in this new honorable task. Klarissa stared back at the others who looked upon her for guidance.

"There is also a boy…a boy that we must help, for he has no path, and all is unknown before him…both to us and to the gods."

II. Two Young Hunters

The land of Sark is a cold, solitary island located in a vast magical sea. It lies forgotten by other kingdoms, a broken land of ice and snow, located between the four winds. It is a land of sleeping power, with cliffs reaching from icy seas up to mountains spotted with black trees made of rock-like bark. These trees are known as kial thierens, and to the people of Sark they are the most precious resource. They provide fire, food, and strands of fiber woven to make clothing. Some of the tribes of Sark regard the trees as holy. They are indigenous to Sark and without them, the Sarkians would not survive. Resting at the foot of a circle of these ancient trees, three travelers sat by a small campfire. Two were children, and one was seemingly an old man.

Kaila was a young girl, only eight years old. She was a huntress, so she was garbed as such. She wore grey wolf fur and clothes fashioned of leather. Her hair was light brown, with strands of blonde peeking through. The child kept her hair in a long braid, which her mother had always helped her with. A fur cap adorned her head. The young huntress lay dreaming now, remembering really. She saw visions of her mother, Khabria, the strongest and most feared huntress in all of Sark. She was beautiful, with long blonde hair and bright blue eyes. Kaila figured that her mother laughed often enough, though few saw it. She loved it when her mother laughed, and especially when they laughed at the same things. Kaila was counted among the lucky ones to witness such a beautiful sound, for it was not often that a huntress had reason to laugh. She was also, unfortunately, one of the only people who could be haunted by it as well, haunted because she would never hear it again unless it were in her dreams.

She remembered that her mother had been fashioning a blade for her. It was not finished yet, but Kaila had been allowed to practice with it. She had yet to kill with it. It was sharp, and created by her mother out of valka bone. Her mother had killed the beast in the ceremonial hunt. Khabria was one of the only women to have killed a valka beast. They were slow-moving, gentle beasts, but when threatened, they were deadly. They are creatures as tall as the trees with long trunks, and massive antlers. One stomp from a valka and a human could be flattened. Many hunters had lost their lives hunting the valka beasts. Khabria had been branded a leader. She had received the mark of the spear piercing the valka on her arm, and given the crown of antlers to adorn her head during her initiation. Kaila had always been proud to have her as a mother, and she had always felt safe that her mother was always there to teach her the ways of hunting.

There were also memories of her step-father, Havink. Even though he was not her real father, he acted as if he were. He showed her how to lay traps, and skin animals. He even taught her how to cook the meat to season it for the best taste. He was actually much better than her real father. Havink knew how to laugh, and how to make Khabria laugh as well. He was always full of stories when night came, and Kaila would often fall asleep curled up with her mother, nestled in her arms, listening to the sound of Havink's voice tell stories of the gods, while surrounded by the orange glow of firelight. She knew happiness and love. They had taught her how to be a strong huntress, and she had always looked forward to the day when she could be initiated as her mother had been. She was remembering all these best moments of her life until...her dream became dark, but then light again as if she was forced back into a world of warmth and glowing firelight. Her dream wouldn't let her relive the recent events, not yet. She remembered her mother, her beauty, her strength, and her teachings. These were things that Kaila could never have taken from her, things which although real and true had been programmed into her dream by the angel watching over her. He knew where her dreams would lead if he were not here, and she deserved sleep without nightmares.

That angel was one of the oldest living creatures, an Orostiro named Slatkin, a child of Saigolai, the god of life, and he was the one who watched over these children. There was Kaila, who needed special care. She was dangerous to herself right now. After all, she had experienced the death of her mother and step-father at the hands of a powerful, evil creature, and the slaying had been ordered by her paternal father, Volkhan, the main tribal leader. She had been saved from death by her half-brother, Galan, but captured and eventually her and her brother had both been saved by three angels. The other two angels, Alexandria and Angelik, had departed to take care of business elsewhere in Sark, but Slatkin stayed with the children. He was looking out for them, making sure that nothing would happen to them, including nightmares. Kaila had not wanted to eat or sleep. She had been staring at the fire, remembering her mother's death, and gripping the carved Valka bone in her hand. She had been swearing to herself that she would not cry, for it was a sign of weakness to the hunters. She did not wish to sound like a whimpering animal, either. She also swore to herself that she would avenge her mother's death. What Volkhan had done to them was unnatural. Yes, her mother may have betrayed him, but not more than he had betrayed Khabria. She vowed to herself that she would kill Volkhan, as she gripped the blade tighter in her hand. That's when she looked up and noticed the old man's blue eyes. As she gazed into them, she had forgotten everything that had happened recently. Comfort overwhelmed her and she soon fell into a deep sleep of dreams that were only of remembering the good things.

Galan slept close by her. He was just a boy, only twelve, but in the tribe of the hunters, who had a short life expectancy, that was considered a man. He wore his dark brown hair shorn off with a brown fur cap adorning his head. He was important in the hunting tribe, the son of Volkhan. Volkhan had many sons, but he was the only one granted the privilege to live in the same abode as his father. He had his own team of sled dogs, and he was sometimes asked to instruct the other hunters. He had failed at this many times, though. Volkhan had accused him of being like his mother far too often, always with a beating to follow. His mother, Khali, was an important woman, being the current wife of Volkhan, but she was also a slave. The only women who were allowed to be equal to the men were the ones who were born to two hunters, a rare occurrence. Many of the women hunters did not make it past the age of ten years. Sometimes they were killed by wild beasts, and other times they would not survive the winters. More often than not they did not survive ceremonies inducting them into the title of hunter. Khanhine, the hunter god, had not been generous to bestowing the title of hunter upon women.

Galan thought it was unfair, but who was he to question the god Khanhine?

His mother was born of the Astrids, another tribe. The hunters think that the Astrids have magical gifts. They can speak directly with the gods, and they are considered of great value in the quest to destroy the khanhine-lupah, creatures who appear to be human, but mock Khanhine, the god of the hunt, by turning into wolves and leading the hunters away from their prey, often to great peril. It is believed that the Astrids can see the true shapes of the khanhine-lupah, whereas others cannot. The women of the tribe are often sought out to be mates to the hunters in the hope that the magical quality will pass down to the hunters, allowing them to rid the world of the khanhine-lupah for good. They are also learned in the magic of healing, and they possess knowledge of the plant life that has long been lost to the hunters. If an Astrid is taken as a mate, she must be trained and broken into the way of the hunters. They are hard women to break, naturally resisting the hunter's way of life. That is the hunter's view.

The Astrid's have a different view, and Galan had been privileged, or cursed, to learn both ways of life. His mother had raised him to speak her language as well as that of the hunters. She sometimes told him stories of her people, and the stories of the gods were always different. The Astrids do not have magical powers. They do have knowledge about the land however, such as how to flavor foods and use the plants for healing. They understand the kial thieren trees and the power locked inside. They can communicate with the gods, but only through stones that are located in the midst of their village. They are only a half-tribe. The women are the Astrids. They live apart from their male relatives, the Wards, who come to visit the women only once each year, during the Lauming, a fertility feast that happens each summer. The males live with their mothers for the first five years, and then they move to the other side of the land. That is so they can learn the wisdom of the gods, for men and women each have gifts, but they are different. Galan learned from his mother that although considered great and powerful, Khanhine is only a lesser god. There are gods with greater gifts, such as Saigolai, the god of life. She always said that Saigolai was powerful enough to kill even Khanhine if he wished, for he brought about life just by thinking it and if he could give it, then he could also take it away. It was Saigolai that paired lovers, and Saigolai that blessed children into being in their mother's womb. He is the greatest of the gods, for he brought all other gods into being.

Galan was given power to choose and decide for himself which one he believed in. He still did not know. For all he knew, there were no gods. There was only survival, and you could choose to survive or choose to die. He had chosen to die earlier, but was granted with not only his life, but his half-sister's. He still wasn't sure why he had saved her. He barely knew her, yet he felt a need to protect her, and he had been willing to die trying to save her...and he still might. He wondered then about his father. Was he still alive? If he was alive, would he be looking for him? Galan hoped so in a way, and yet, he hoped that his father was dead. He was terrified of what his father would do if he ever found him. He would be considered a traitor...and Galan had seen many times what happened to those who betrayed the hunters.

He watched his sister, thinking deeply about what to do. He was surely an outcast now. He would never be able to go back home to his father, not after saving Kaila. They would kill him. An even worse thought was that they would kill Kaila. For some reason this made him angry. She had done nothing to them. She was just a girl that had watched as her parents were murdered in front of her. Galan thought about how he would have felt if that were him instead of her. He loved his mother. He didn't think he could live if he had seen her die in such a way. He admitted that Khabria and Havink's death had disturbed him, and they weren't even his parents.

After many hours of thinking, Galan lay down by the fire and drifted off to sleep as well, while Slatkin, the Orostiro, sat wide awake. He wore only a long black coat buttoned from his neck to his knees and a fur wrapped around his shoulders. His other clothes were too ripped and torn to repair so he had left them in the woods. He watched over the two children with the utmost care. He monitored their dreams and all of their emotions. His quest was vital for them, but also for the well-being of Sark. At the moment, the objective was simple. He had to go back for Galan's mother. Volkhan would be coming for them all. Slatkin was unsure of how exactly the hunter would reappear, but he knew that it would happen. Volkhan's evil soul was too useful for the Shadow to cast aside. He would use the hunter, twist his sense of humanity, and mold him into something that only pure evil could conceive. He may appear human when he returned, but then again he may not. Slatkin would have to try to stay alert, aware. He had to be ready for anything. He had to be ready when Volkhan gained his new power. That is what was happening. He could feel the Shadow getting stronger, swelling and silently building itself up. The evil was growing and it was only just beginning. The humans could probably not understand what was about to happen, but Slatkin could sense it. He had lived it before.

Being an Orostiro, one of the first children born to Saigolai, he was alive in the time before the world was made, and one of the first to cross the threshold into the kingdom of mankind. He had seen many things in his eons of living, and many times, he saw things repeat themselves. It was a pattern of life. Humans would thrive, and then they would make mistakes, only to forget them and have them repeated every generation. As long as they had a lesson to learn, he was here to guard them, to teach them, to reward and punish them as necessary. That was why he was made. If there was any creature that could protect these children, it was him...but he had his doubts. There had been many times that he had forgotten his purpose. Many times that he had lived with men for so long that he counted himself one of them. He could not let that happen again. He had to do this task. There was no room for errors, no time for distractions. The Shadow was growing, and if Slatkin failed in his quest, then many more than just these two children would perish.

He attuned his senses to everything around them. Every movement was captured in detail by his eyes and his hearing could catch sounds for miles, whether it was the rustling of leaves far above their heads, or the barking of wolves away in the distance. The aroma of the burning logs on the campfire was almost overpowering. He sat staring into the darkness, wondering in what way Nometheog, the Shadow god, would choose to present himself this time. The god of the Void had often visited the land of men. Each time he came he had new devices at hand, some clever way of winning the hearts and souls of men. Each time Slatkin had been there protecting them, but each time it had been a new challenge. Always though,

Saigolai had prevailed and men were granted new lives, better lives. His night was spent in guessing how the evil would present itself. Then in the morning the children awoke, and he put all his efforts into helping them.

Kaila awoke slowly. A quivering frown lined her face, but she did not cry. She wouldn't let herself. It was a sign of weakness to the hunters, and so she bit the corners of her lips to keep the tears back as she realized that she had only been sleeping and the memory of her mother was just a dream. She quickly walked away with the excuse that she had to relieve her bladder, but she was gone for far longer than was necessary. She took the few minutes to stop her tears. It made her angry at herself. She hated that she was so small, and not yet trained like her mother. She would train, though. She promised herself. She would get Galan to teach her. Surely, he would help her in her quest. She looked at the knife again. She would use this. It was made with her mother's hand. The perfect tool to slit a throat...she jumped when she realized that Galan was walking toward her. She kept her head down, hoping that he did not see her reddened face.

"I thought you had gotten lost," he said, "quit trying to run away." Kaila did not answer. She was afraid her voice would quiver and give away her emotions. So, she just shook her head. She bit her lip so hard that she could taste blood welling in her mouth. Galan wanted to say something to her, but he couldn't find the words. He looked around for a moment, then reached out and gave her a nudge on the shoulder. "Well, come on, we have to leave now. It's no longer safe here. The old man doesn't feel that we should linger anywhere for too long and especially you by yourself. You need to stay with us so that we can protect you."

Again, she could not find it in herself to speak, so she nodded her head in reply. She turned and followed him back to the camp, spitting her blood on the ground as they walked.

They packed up when they returned, and Slatkin destroyed all evidence that they had camped there. By this time a pale dawn had stretched out across the land. Beneath the boughs of the kial thierens, the land seemed dark, but the snow had turned from a shadowy gray hue, to a pale blue. The sky was barely visible in the bit of forest that they traveled in. The branches of the tall, rock solid trees intertwined above their heads, giving the false sense of being in a cave, though it was a windy cave. The shifting winds of Sark whistled a low, hollow tune through the cracks in the branches and the three travelers moved on toward a safer place.

Slatkin stopped when he knew that the children would need to rest. This time, they found a hollowed kial thieren tree to rest in. Slatkin left the children there while he went to find food for them. He walked out to a clearing nearby. The sun shone down through a break in the clouds, bright and blinding, but in the midst of the clearing grew a rare pink flower. It grew only in places with full sunlight and well drained soil. The angel only knew this because of Belle's teachings. She was the gravity of all his thoughts but the peril of his quest. He knew that to love her was a terrible, unnatural thing. She was a mortal earth witch. His father had forbidden such things. Slatkin felt guilt even now, so far away from her. He knew he should be concentrating on a plan, but he was thinking of her more often now that he was away from home. She lived with him, worked beside him, and was a constant temptation.

He tried to turn his thoughts away, but they always came back to her. Everything about her captivated him, from the varied colors he saw in her soul and her earthen striking beauty to her unnatural intelligence and plant lore. She knew everything about the land of Sark. She seemed to have some unexplained connection to the land. To her, nature was simple. For every living thing, there was a season, and for every season there was a time to grow and a time to rest. The Orostiro had never been able to see the world in this way. Everything was so complicated for him, especially the nature of humanity. Nothing was simple for him because the very nature of mankind was so chaotic.

Slatkin walked over to pluck the pale pink flower from the stem. It had many uses. Belle had once taught him that the flower itself was said to relieve fear and anxiety when boiled in water. The vapor had a calming effect. The leaves could be combined with the kial flowers to create a salve that would heal open wounds, and the stems could be chewed to heal a sore throat. She shared this with him, knowledge that his own father had never cared to pass down to him. He wondered why. Why was he kept from this when something so simple could help so many? It was his duty to protect these humans. Shouldn't he know of it? Belle had said it was because he didn't need it.

"Your way of healing is within you. Perhaps Saigolai thought it insignificant to you, since you can already do everything the flower can. You see, he made it for my kind, not yours. We are the ones he meant to use it. That is why we have the knowledge and you do not." Slatkin smiled at the thought of Belle. He wanted to see her now, to feel her. As quickly as the sun had shown down upon the meadow it vanished, and once again the white snow was a blue hue, instead of the pure white it had been moments before. Snowflakes began to drift from the sky, slow and twirling in the gusts of bitter wind. He tucked the bloom away in his coat pocket and stood listening. Far in the distance he could hear dogs barking. There was a sound of rushing water not too far away. Birds cawed lazily from the tree tops, the wind whistled from the branches, but nothing more. They would be safe here for now.

He made his way back to the hollow tree. As he approached the tree, he listened for conversation from the children, but there was none. He ducked his way inside to find Kaila safely nestled in Galan's arms, her head lay on his shoulder and she was sleeping soundly for the moment. Galan looked tired, but he was wide awake.

"She's freezing," he said. It sounded like an excuse for the show of affection towards his sister.

Slatkin smiled at the thought. It was comical. Humans were a constant puzzle, always hiding the very things that they wanted to show. "Thank you for looking out for her."

"So did you catch anything?" Galan asked, ignoring Slatkin's comment. The dark angel shook his head. "No, but I will. We will not stop here for too much longer. We can reach our current destination by nightfall if we do not tarry long. Besides, there is nothing around here except birds, and I am not fond of eating the kraelvins.

"I'm not picky," said Galan.

"Well, I am. Kraelvins are not meant for eating, they are different than other birds." Slatkin thought of Carmina, the nephilim that was attendant to the queen. He could picture the widening of her blue eyes and the gasp of horror that she would sound if she knew that he was traveling with someone who would eat one of her friends, the messengers from other realms.

"Well, we are resting here only. There will be plenty to eat tonight. We will be to your home by then, Galan. Your mother will have Valka stew and there will be more than the four of us can eat. She is still expecting your father and the rest of the hunters to be there tonight."

"I forget that she doesn't know..." Galan's words trailed off. The days since he had left his home seemed like an eternity to him now. So much had happened. He had swallowed his words before he could give voice to his thoughts. He now faced telling the events to his mother, and explaining how he was now an outcast among the tribe. He had put not only his sister in danger, but his mother too. His arm tightened around Kaila. After thinking about it, he thought that his mother would understand but the thought still lingered that she wouldn't. What if she would not let him go? Worse yet, what if she let him go, but didn't come with him? He didn't think that he could find it within himself to let her stay alone in that cabin, knowing that his father may still be alive. The first place that Volkhan would go to would be the cabin. As much as he wished his father would come back and everything would be normal, he also wished that his father was indeed dead and would never bother them again. If he was alive, perhaps he could possibly take his mother somewhere safe. They could go far away, where his father would never find them.

"We'll be there this evening," Slatkin said, interrupting the boy's thoughts. "If I were you, I would rest now, while you can." Galan never questioned why the angel seemed to know everything that he was feeling and thinking. He was beginning not to question any strange occurrence that involved the old man. After all, he had seen him as a beast and had tried to kill him, only to find out later that it was the beast that had saved him from a terrible fate. He leaned back and soon drifted off into a restful sleep, with the angel watching over him. Slatkin decided now was the time for him to also rest. His back and chest still ached from the wounds he had received while saving Galan from his father in the barren lands. He had begun to heal, but the pain was still there. He tried to ignore it, but he could not. He gathered that they would be safe for a little while. Rest would help the wound to heal. He lay down, and immediately he drifted into a light sleep, one filled with dreams of dread and longing. He longed for Belle, but there was so much he had to accomplish before he could see her again. Never again could he risk hurting her. Never again. He had to stay away until the longing subsided. That was the only way to keep her safe. It was good that he had work to keep him busy. While he was working it was easier to cast aside the part of him that felt human, easier to rid himself of the temptations that he knew were counterproductive to his quest.

III. Volkhan's Awakening

Volkhan awoke in pain. It was pain that he could not have imagined in his worst nightmares. It was pain so excruciating that he could not hear himself yell. Breathing was only done with great effort. He felt as if his chest had been crushed and his ribs were piercing his organs. It was both dull ache and sharp, stabbing pains. It spread through his body like a slow, freezing ice creeping through his veins. When he tried to move his body, the pain intensified. He could see nothing, just a great expanse of darkness that gave him no comfort from his pain. From somewhere far away, a voice spoke.

"He'll come around soon, and then we will see what his usefulness is." The voice was familiar, but not enough for Volkhan to place it and he didn't care to. He only wanted the pain to end. The voice spoke again, the same, but yet different, "*Yes, his heart is black. He will seek revenge...*" there was laughter: cold, cackling, insane laughter. "*I am amused by the possibilities! Just imagine what he'll think of when he discovers the betrayal!*" More laughter followed. The noise increased the pain and

Volkhan was sure that he was dying, if not, he now wished it. The pain increased until he could bear it no more. He was soon passed out, floating in a vast darkness that lay somewhere between life and death.

Upon waking a second time, intense heat flowed through him. He thought he was on fire, his whole body was burning. He felt fire everywhere, not just on his skin, but it was within him, boiling in his veins. He was inhaling it and exhaling it. He was sure that he was screaming it. He heard his own scream, his own cough, a terrible gurgling sound in his throat. He heard it, but was unsure if it was in his own thoughts or if it had really happened. All he was certain of was the burning that wrapped him in agony. Suddenly a hand clasped his throat, holding him on the place where he lay. Through the searing heat and pain he was able to discern a figure. It was the weapon, the woman that had killed the Valka beast. Her strength held him in place, though he knew he was squirming, kicking, writhing beneath her arm. She held him steady, and the fire intensified. His vision blurred to a blinding white light.

The woman leaned down and spoke to him. "You must endure the pain. It is your new life being created. Shekley has given you this new life. You are immortal now, a weapon of the Shadow. Like me, you are indebted to him. You will do as he says, and if you fight against him, you will remain in this state, this unbearable state of wishing you could die...for you cannot die anymore. The dark god wants you to accept his pain as a cleansing of your old self. You are no longer the man Volkhan, but a hunter who stalks the Shadow's prey. Accept this pain and you will be rewarded beyond what you can imagine!"

Volkhan heard himself shouting. "I'll do anything...I'll give him whatever he wants!" With those words, the pain intensified to a final climax and then Volkhan was sleeping.

When he awoke for the third time, there was an exhilarating chill all around him. With each breath, there was a tingling thrill that shuddered throughout him. It was the breath of new life. He stared down at his body. He was naked, but he did not recognize parts of himself. Metal patches were worked over parts of him. His ribs were covered in the metal, and parts of his legs and arms. He reached down to his ribs to feel of the metallic material that was now part of him, but then he stopped to look at his hands. There were no hands, just metallic claws. They were large and bulky, but they looked sharp and animalistic. He rubbed them together and smiled when he realized how well he could feel with them. If he could not see them as large metal paws, he would never have known they were not his original hands. Everything felt natural. He slid off the table he had been laying on into a clumsy stand, he felt lightheaded, and there were halos around his vision. He looked around and realized that there were others lying on tables nearby. He felt disoriented, displaced and yet light and refreshed. He felt of his face, somehow changed, but he couldn't know exactly how without seeing his reflection.

He stared around the room and realized that there were other tables in the room. Hunters lay atop them all. He recognized the others on the tables only by faint traces of resemblance. He looked back at his own table. There were clothes on shelves beneath it. He reached out to touch them, looking at them. They were his. He remembered that. He reached for his pants with his new paws and he slipped them on.

Things were starting to come back to him as he fumbled with the fastenings of his clothes. He remembered his son stabbing a beast and then the beast had knocked him away from the fight. "I have to find that creature," Volkhan said, as he slipped on his boots, "and my son."

He walked then to the others, looking at them on the tables. He saw comrades there, but he also saw creatures. He stared at them. Perhaps his son was here. Maybe he killed the beast and made it here after all. He checked them all, but Galan was not among them. A door opened then, and the arms dealer walked into the room.

"My son," said Volkhan. "I need to find him," he said. His own voice sounded more like a growl to him.

"He's with the beast. You need to find it. He's the one that has taken your son, and he took the little girl, too. You must find the beast and kill him! You can bring the boy and the girl back to me." He knew that he should ask the man more questions. What kind of weapons did he now possess? What could he now do? Was he like the woman that had held him to the table? The words failed him, and instead of a desire for knowledge, he felt an urgency to *Find the beast and kill him. Find the beast and kill him...bring the boy and the girl back to me...* it repeated in his head, a new obsession.

"Two will go with you," Shekley said, motioning to the open doorway. Volkhan stepped through the threshold into another room, where what used to be Haz and Malik stood waiting. Haz had changed most recognizably. His whole face had been changed. Instead of a new jaw, he had received an entire snout with sharp, metal tusks protruding dangerously from his jaws. He looked like half boar, half man. His eyes glowed red and fierce. They were angry, malicious eyes. Malik, a tall, lanky hunter, looked mostly unchanged. The largest difference was his hair, or lack thereof. He was completely bald, but hardly changed except for small splashes of metal lining his face and vein like traces of the material running throughout his skin. Volkhan, if he could have seen himself would have seen a man with wolfish features, complete with metal teeth including sharp, pronounced canines. The three hunters stared at each other for a moment, taking in the strange effects.

"Are you ready to see what we can do?" Malik asked, when he spoke, there was a wavering in his voice, almost as if he was humming or buzzing.

Volkhan nodded. Haz grinned a terrifying grin with his new snout. They looked for the man and the other weapon, the woman, but they were nowhere around. Volkhan felt new instincts awakening in him. Even though he had not been far into the complex of Shekley's stronghold, he seemed to feel his way around without needing a map, or directions. A force unknown urged him forward and guided him where to go to exit. They walked through several halls, and down a staircase, then out of the main entrance. Volkhan paused to stare out at the expanse of black sand surrounding them in the blinding sun. He was calculating how far to his cabin.

"We'll travel quicker now than we did before," Haz said. Volkhan nodded.

Now that he was away from the stronghold, with a breeze blowing, he thought of his son. "My boy would have gotten away," he reasoned. "I don't care what the man said, he would have gotten away and he'll have gone back home to his Mama. We'll go northwest, to my cabin."

"No," said Malik, his new voice sounded with the strange buzzing. "I think you're wrong. It's just West, not Northwest."

"How would you know?" asked Haz.

"I smell their blood," said Malik.

Volkhan thought for a moment. "You go West, and we'll head Northwest, then. If you find them, bring them to me."

Malik laughed loudly. Buzzing erupted from his throat instead of laughter. "I might decide to, but they smell tasty, Volkhan. Their blood..." Malik sniffed the air as if a pleasant meal had been placed before them. "It's enticing!"

Volkhan roared with a rage and wrapped his sharp metal claws around Malik's throat. He felt them for the first time with his anger attached. "You WILL bring him to me ALIVE!"

Malik raised his index finger to Volkhan's eye. The end of his fingertip was a long, sharp needle.

Volkhan pushed himself away. "You're repulsive! The boy is a hunter, one of our own!" exclaimed Volkhan.

Malik shook his head, a wide smile spread across his face. "I am like no other! I am newly made, a creature of Nometheog!" He spread his arms in his newfound freedom. "No longer do I toil in the brush for Khanhine...no, I smell the sweet life force of the world. I will taste it. I will taste it until there is no more and Nometheog will relish in my victory over it!"

A deep growl was emanating from within Volkhan's chest. He glared at the former hunter as Malik stood laughing, buzzing with delight.

"You promised to come with me. If you will not help me kill the beast and deliver my son to Nometheog, then I suggest you turn back now!"

Volkhan looked at Haz. "Well, are you with him or me?"

Haz thought for a moment. "I'm with you Volkhan. You're right. The boy would have gone home if he got away."

Then Malik laughed again. zzz...zzz...His throat vibrated, buzzing when he laughed. "He may not have gotten away. Have you considered that?"

"He's smarter than you give him credit for, Malik."

Malik walked up to Volkhan, and stared him in the eyes. "He's already a man, and he's still just as soft as his mother. He's weak."

A growl erupted from Volkhan as he shoved Malik away with new found strength. "Like I said, he's smarter than you give him credit for and certainly stronger than you!"

"I'm heading West!" Malik exclaimed defiantly. "You go where you want, but when I reach them, I will taste their blood! I will feast on them, and leave a trail of their innards for you to follow." He turned to leave. "If you go Northwest, I will reach them first!" he taunted as he walked away, heading west, leaving them to listen to the terrible buzzing sound emitted from his throat as he laughed again.

Haz looked at Volkhan. "You think he's telling the truth?" Volkhan didn't say anything. He stared at Malik's back and wondered to himself whether or not he could be wrong, but he was listening to his own reasoning.

"My boy stabbed the beast with his sword. I saw it before the creature knocked me away. He could have easily taken down the beast. He didn't kill it, but I'm sure he got away. The man is wrong about it." He nodded his head with certainty. "He's back at the cabin. He was eyeing the girl earlier. He probably took her for his own." Volkhan nodded. "They're back at the cabin. I'm sure of it!"

"Then let us not waste any more time!" said Haz.

Volkhan smiled wickedly. "Soon we will present my son to Nometheog!" The two hunters walked forward confidently, excited with thoughts of victory.

IV. The Queen

Victor slept soundly at Celeste's side, more content than he had been in the seven years since she had been missing. His arm was curled around her, not letting go of her even in his sleep. Her long, black curls fell around them both like a blanket. Celeste had slept soundly for most of the day, feeling a safety and reassurance that she had missing for years, but she could not rest for long. She had awakened much too early with a lot on her mind. For several nights, she had not slept well. Her dreams were filled with wishes and unfulfilled assignments. She had recently been rescued from the land of Shea, where she had been held captive by Kristiniva, goddess of the sky. She had been there for seven long years, separated from the people she loved, the god that she served, and her powers had slowly been drained, taken by the goddess. Her powers were tied to the people of the land, and since her power is love, her land had suffered in her absence. The land that she was held captive in was not on any map that she had ever seen. It existed on another plane of time, separate from all the other lands. Now that she was back, there was a long list of things to do to rebuild her kingdom. Nothing was the same as she had left it.

She looked over at her husband, who still slept soundly, and realized that part of his face had a red tint to it. When he had saved her, he had been returned to his full power, that of justice. She had been pained to discover that in order for her to be saved, he had to take all of her pain from the last seven years. That included being brutally beaten and burned, while in the last days of pregnancy, by a group of hunters that had betrayed them when they were the rulers of Sark. She wondered why it had to be him. Why must he share her misery? He was the last one, other than her daughter, that she would have chosen. She leaned down and placed a light kiss on his cheek. The redness lightened. He stirred slightly, clutching her more tightly in his sleep. She pulled the blankets closer to him and placed his hand around them then she slid out of the bed reaching for her dressing gown which she pulled on, along with her warm, fur slippers.

The breaking lines of dusk were not yet in the sky. It was still early in the evening, yet she could sleep no longer. She felt things, a calling. There were so many of her subjects calling for her gift that she was overwhelmed with things to do at the moment. The first thing, though, was to get rid of the sickening smell of the goddesses' sky flowers that still hung about her. She could smell the scents of Shea still clinging to her strands of hair and skin. When mixed with the smell of the kial wood burning in the hearth, she felt nauseous. Before even leaving the room, she reached for the red Shean robe. The scent of it was disgusting and it had steadily spread through her chambers like a disease.

She reached into the pocket and retrieved a small item. She had kept it with her ever since Arik the elf had given it to her. It was a small vial of what he had called endless dust. It had the ability to cure almost any ailment. He had given it to her to cure her burns, but now that she was home, her healing was complete. She knew that its uses were many and that it was probably more valuable than any of the jewels that she owned. She walked over to her jewelry boxes. Many of them looked untouched since her disappearance. She reached for one of the smaller boxes, one with a key in it. She unlocked it and emptied out the jewels. She then searched her drawers for a sash.

She pulled out a silver one and wrapped the little vial of endless dust in it, then stowed it in the box. She then took the key, and for the moment, placed it on the mantle above her fireplace. She would find a better place for both of them later. Next she picked up the robe. She would have to burn it. She hated it, the garb of her slavery in Shea. She pulled open the door to her bedroom, and saw that Carmina, her attending lady, was in the sitting room building a fire. She was startled when the queen entered.

She quickly stood and curtsied. The gesture seemed strange after so long, but also awkward because of Carmina's size. She was a nephilim, standing seven feet tall.

"Good evening, my queen!"

Celeste smiled. "It's been too long since I have heard that! I'm going to have to get used to it all over again." Although she had been home for several nights, the old, every day customs of being queen were an adjustment after being a slave for so long. It was like stepping back into a past that was a dream, yet everything was new and different, not like she left it at all, and she was surprised to hear things like "my queen" and "your grace". It's like she had forgotten a part of herself that used to bear those names but now suddenly remembered that she belonged to them after that part of herself had died.

"And it has been too long since my lips have uttered it!" They both smiled.

"Shall I dress you?" Carmina offered.

"No," said Celeste. "I want you to go and collect soaps and oils. Strong ones, ones scented with things native to this kingdom. There is a stench of sky flowers stuck to me, and I must rid myself of this before I can even concentrate on the tasks at hand. I will bathe in the hot spring, and while I'm bathing, you may collect clothes for me. If you can find riding breeches, then that will be the best thing. I do not want dresses and robes. I will be doing a lot of riding and walking in the days to come."

"Yes, my queen!" Carmina replied.

Celeste held the robe up. "I need to burn this," she said.

"Should I do it?" Carmina asked.

"No," the queen said shaking her head. "No, I will do it after I bathe. I want to watch as it burns. I want to make sure that I am rid of my slavery for good."

"It must have been terrible!" said Carmina, tears of sympathy and guilt welled in her eyes. "I should have been more prepared!"

"No, Carmina. Do not blame yourself." Celeste just looked at her for a moment; her green eyes dim with the memory. "No one is to blame, and besides that, we cannot dwell on the past. If anything, we must learn from it and move on to happier days. She paused for a moment before continuing. "Kristiniva has paid for what she did to me, but she has done a horrible injustice to my people! It may take years to overcome, but I will put the slavery behind me, and think of it as little as possible. There is much to do. There are many of my subjects that need my gift and it is time that I cleansed myself of this past, and move forward. I must rebuild my kingdom, and reclaim the things that have been lost."

"As always, I offer my services. Is there anything I can do to aid you, my queen?" Carmina asked.

"Of course, but the first step is the soaps. I MUST rid myself of this odor!" She then turned, and left her chambers, heading toward the hot springs.

When she reached the hot springs, Carmina was not far behind with Belle, the castle's cook. They had an array of oils and soaps for the queen.

"Evening, m'lady!" exclaimed Belle. Her bright red hair was hidden in a kerchief. She seemed older and more worn than Celeste remembered.

"Good evening, Belle!" she said back with a smile. "I want anything made from kial wood or flowers, and if you have anything that smells as powerful and mixes well, then I will take that also," she said.

Belle laid a basket of oils and dried herbs on the table. "I have Baika vine. The leaves will be potent." She said, pulling out a bottle of dried leaves.

"Perfect," Celeste said. She stepped into the hot spring and Belle sprinkled the leaves into the spring. The aroma was instant. The smell was clean and minty. "Carmina," said Celeste. "I want you to cut my hair as I bathe. It may be the only way to truly get rid of the flowery smell."

"But...my queen..." she gasped.

"Please, do this for me," said Celeste. "It will not take it long to grow back.

Carmina and Belle both shared stunned looks, but then the nephilim turned to leave. "I will go gather a cutting tool," she said.

"Belle, have you prepared breakfast?" The queen asked.

"It is cooking as we speak," she said. "There's really not much left in the stores, but Carmina did manage to kill a small rabbit. I've seasoned it, so we've got that cooking over the fire. There's also some stew made from kial roots. But that's all I had."

"That will be perfect," Celeste smiled.

A small smile creased its way onto Belle's face.

"By the way," said Celeste. "How is the boy...Evingh?"

"He's...still sleeping, m'lady. He always lies late until I awaken him. Even then, I'm never sure if he's awake."

Celeste nodded. "He is, in a way." She sensed Belle's uncertainty and despair about how to take care of the boy. "He will never forget the kindness and the care that you have given him, Belle. You may never see it, or understand it, but he needs you. You have something that none of us can give him and we all will have you to thank one day."

"What exactly did Slatkin do to him?" she heard herself asking aloud.

Celeste looked at her for a moment, her smile faded and her expression turned serious. "I'm not sure. All I know is that he is troubled, reliving things in his mind. Horrible things. He is stuck in a never ending nightmare that is of his own making and although you care for him, he can only emerge from the nightmare when his soul is ready to. Nothing can make him truly wake from it until then."

Belle frowned a little.

"Don't be discouraged, Belle, he will come around with time, and with your care," the queen reassured.

Just then, the door opened, and Carmina entered with shears. "Are you ready, my queen?" she asked, frowning.

"Yes," Celeste smiled. She leaned her head against the stones that lined the spring and pulled her hair out. Carmina hesitated, but then began to cut. Layers of black curls fell to the stone floor as she cut. Tears filled the nephilim's eyes. She didn't know why, but it just seemed wrong that she was cutting some part of her queen, even if the queen requested it.

Celeste smiled. "It will be okay, Carmina. You will see, it will not take long at all to grow back, and when it does, it will not have that obnoxious scent in it." The nephilim nodded, sniffling. When all the layers had been cut, the queen sat in the bath with her hair shorn off next to her head. She smiled up at Carmina.

"Now you can take the hair with my Shean robe outside, but do not burn it yet. I want to be there. When it is removed from the castle, come back here."

Carmina nodded. "Yes, my queen," she said.

When the other two had left, and she was sure that she was alone, she used the soaps and the oils to vigorously scrub the remaining traces of Shea from her skin and hair. She submerged herself in the water, head and all, and let the purity of the hot spring wash away the feeling of Kristiniva's hand brushing her face, the scents that blew through the castle and the memory of how the red Shean robe swept over her skin. They were all sensations that were, to her, slavery, and as the water swept past her it seemed to wash it all away.

When Carmina returned with the clothes, Celeste was more than ready. She stepped out of her bath and dried herself, refusing help from Carmina.

"Could you find anything?" she asked.

"Well, I was able to find some riding breeches. I'm afraid that they've been in the trunk for a long time, but they seem to be in decent shape." The pair that she pulled out was black and woven from kial fibers. Celeste smiled.

"They are perfect," she said.

"Then there's this," Said Carmina. She reached out and pulled out a grey tunic. "I thought that after wearing that red robe for so long, you wouldn't want to wear red."

Celeste smiled. "Thank you, Carmina. It is still the color of our kingdom, but the black and grey will suit me perfect for what I'm about to do."

Carmina then added a black riding corset, black riding boots, a long gray riding coat, and black gloves. When the queen was fully dressed, they made their way to the dining hall, where Victor was already waiting. When he saw his wife, Victor stood up and walked to her.

"Celeste?" he asked, reaching out to touch her shorn off hair. She smiled.

"I know it's drastic, but it will probably be back in a week anyway. Victor, I had to get that stench of sky flowers out of it!"

He nodded and kissed her. "Well I'm glad. It was atrocious." She giggled.

"That it was!" she exclaimed, lightheartedly. Just then, Belle entered with a small tray.

"Breakfast is served," she said, as she placed it on the table.

"Ah!" exclaimed Celeste, inhaling its pleasant aroma "This is something that I'm ready for!"

They then sat down to the small meal of rabbit and kial stew that Belle had prepared for them. Carmina pulled Celeste's chair out and pushed it back in before seating herself. While the three of them ate, Belle left to awaken Evingh.

After her breakfast, Celeste was ready to burn her past. She stared down at the robe and the pile of hair lying on the stack of wood in the snow. Victor was there with her, the red color had returned to the right side of his face. Carmina and Belle were there also.

She walked forward with the torch in her hand and carefully lit the fire. Her eyes stung as she did so. She was ready to be rid of this. As the flames slowly caught and danced, she smiled. Partly in prayer to Saigolai, and partly in anger at Kristiniva, she spoke.

"May this flame send its' smoke far into the sky. May it go so far as to reach Shea. I wish for Kristiniva to know of the destruction of her magic. I want her to smell her sky flowers smothering in the scents of Sark. May the Kial smoke rise, so that she knows that I am free, and my people will know love again. They will know it, and she will not. She who steals emotions, so that she may feel! Never again will she steal love!" She raised the torch to the sky as the smoke blackened in rolling clouds, and the fires sputtered with sparks of green and blue. With the torch held high, she said louder, "Hear this Kristiniva, and weep with the knowledge: my gift is mine, and something that is

49

freely given. I could have blessed you. I could have given you everything that you tried to steal, but because it was taken instead of given, I choose to keep it from you and until the time comes when you can graciously and unselfishly accept it, I will keep it from you!" The torch lowered and she felt Victor's arm around her shoulders. She leaned into him, resting against him.

When there was nothing left except ashes and charred wood, she dropped the torch to the ground, and turned to embrace her husband. "I will be rid of it all, I am determined."

He held her close, "We *will* be rid of it, and I will seek justice for the wrongdoings done to you by the hunters. We will build the kingdom once more and it will be stronger than before."

V. Cabin Burning

Slatkin awoke before the children, but felt a panic sweep over him as he realized that they had all slept for far too long. The air had changed. They were no longer safe. The howling of wolves could be heard close by. The kraelvins were quiet, and the wind was from the East. It was a dry wind, a warm wind. It was not a good sign, not for a Sarkian winter. The shadows cast by the trees seemed ominous now, and any appearance of sun had been smothered by deep grey clouds. It was hard to tell the time, but night was quickly approaching. He woke the children, and they gathered what few items they had, and left to go to Galan's home.

Kaila still seemed tired and dazed, and both children were weak from hunger, but Slatkin urged them on. "We will be there soon, and your mother will be pleased to see you, Galan. We will freeze if we stay out too much longer."

"I'm surprised you're not already frozen," he said with a red nose. "How can you walk so long in the snow, without any boots for your feet?" he asked.

Slatkin just smiled. He had lost his shoes and clothes during his last transformation, all except for his long black coat and a shaggy black valka fur. "The angels aren't like humans, Galan. We can do many things that you cannot. If we had to worry over so many insignificant things, then we would have no time to tend to you mortals," Slatkin stated, as they continued the walk to the cabin. Slatkin realized that the dogs he had heard barking earlier in the day were Galan's dogs. They had found their way back home with the sled. Khali, Galan's mother, was mourning, thinking that her husband and son were dead. When she had last seen them, they were riding away with the evil man and his demon. Wherever he led them, she was certain that it was to no good end. They were certainly dead. Why else would the dogs come back without the owners?

They were close enough now that the two children could see the candle light flickering from inside the cabin. Khali had a fire burning in her hearth, and she had many candles lit. When Galan spotted his house, he ran for the last short distance to his door, and he pushed it open with so much force that he almost fell as he passed the threshold.

Khali was quick to run to meet him, reaching out to her son to embrace him. The team of sled dogs were all barking and pawing at Galan, relieved to see that he had come home. They all looked up at him with wagging tails.

"You came back!" she exclaimed as she held him close to her.

Galan wiped the sting from his eyes, thankful that his father did not see. He couldn't help that he was overwhelmed at seeing his mother. There was so much to tell her that he didn't know where to begin. Slatkin stood outside with Kaila. She wanted to cry, too, but she bit her lip again. She felt overwhelming jealousy. She wanted to hold to her mother the way that he did, but she could not, and she was enraged by that thought. How dare he do this in front of her, when she had no mother to embrace! She gripped her blade, but then the thought occurred to her that the blade must kill Volkhan first. It was he who killed her mother, not Galan...

Slatkin knelt down, and looked her in the eyes. "If she asks us in, you can choose to stay outside, and I will remain with you, Kaila," he said.

She looked up at him, pondered what he said, and then moved forward. She had made up her mind. She would go inside. It was warm and dry in there and she needed to rest. Her head hurt from trying to just put aside all the memories of what had happened. She wanted to sleep and dream, so that she could see her mother again.

Slatkin followed her and they stopped at the threshold of the door. Galan broke away from his mother, wiped his eyes with the back of his hand and motioned toward them. "Mother, it's Kaila and Slatkin. He..." Galan swallowed his words. Now that it came to it, it was harder than he thought it would be. When he tried to tell her all that had happened there was a knot of fear in his stomach. There was no way he could bring himself to explain what had happened to them. "He saved us," he finally said. "I saved Kaila..." there was a pause in his words as he struggled with his emotions, "and we have to leave...I have betrayed Volkhan..." he hung his head as he said the words and breathed heavily. "He'll kill me if we don't go." A deep frown lined his face.

Khali held her son, she wanted to weep for him but she looked at him smiling. She reached out wiping the tears from his eyes. She spoke in Astrid. "Hush now son. Calm down. You are with me now, and Saigolai has favored you. He'll not let anyone harm you." She reached into her sleeve and tugged at a stone that was attached to a leather bracelet. When it came close to Galan, it glowed like a fiery ember. "Saigolai protects you, Galan," she said to him. Slatkin's expression became amused at her words.

She guided her son to a table, and she wrapped a grey fur around his shoulders. She reached out to caress his face and then she turned to the two at the door. "Come inside and join us," she said in a thick accent, motioning with her arms for them to come inside to the table. "There is more than enough for us all to eat. Come rest!" she exclaimed. Slatkin and Kaila stepped through the threshold and he closed the door behind them. The warmth from the fire wrapped itself around them. By the time they made it to the table, Khali was already walking to the table balancing four bowls of valka stew. She motioned for them to sit down and she placed the bowls in front of her guests. Kaila started to tip her bowl to eat, but Slatkin grabbed her hand and smiled as he shook his head.

"Not yet," he said. Khali went to get a loaf of bread for them and as she sat, Khali and Galan bowed their heads as Khali blessed the food in the tradition of the Astrids. When her blessing was said, Slatkin released Kaila's hand. He nodded to her then, signaling that it would be okay to eat. The young girl sipped the stew quickly, it burned where she had bit her lips, but she sipped hungrily. Her appetite was finally coming to her. She didn't remember the last time she had eaten without being forced. She was the first to finish, and Khali was quick to give her a second bowl, and more bread, which Kaila ate just as quickly. Slatkin noticed that Khali watched her son intently throughout the meal, questions forming in her mind.

When they had all finished, Khali sang gently to herself while she cleared away the remainder of their meal. Kaila wandered away from the table and lay down on a pile of furs. She was soon asleep with Galan's dogs resting around her. Galan gathered leftovers to feed the dogs. Slatkin sat waiting patiently for Khali to ask the things that she was wondering. When she had her work done, she walked over to him and held out the same bracelet that she had held to her son, and as she held it close to Slatkin, one of the stones lit up a bright white, and seemed to hum with a musical tone. Galan turned from his dogs and stared with interest. Khali nodded her head.

"You are protecting my son," she stated, with approval in her voice.

"Yes," Slatkin reassured.

Khali sat down and held her hand out to Galan. "Come and tell me what has happened. What did you do to Volkhan?"

Galan swallowed. The knot in his throat came back, and the food he just ate felt like it wanted to come back up. He glanced at Slatkin who was nodding his head. He felt himself walking over to sit down by his mother. Her hand rested smoothly on his back, warm and comforting. He took a deep breath and began the story. He told her about how Volkhan and the strange man had ordered the killing of Kaila's parents, and how the unnatural woman had grown weapons to slay them. He told her how Kaila had been ordered dead, but then been saved because of him. Then he explained how the woman killed the Valka beast, and how they had all ended up following the stranger into the barren lands. He explained how Volkhan had ordered him to kill the beast that attacked them, and how he had failed, only to be saved by the same beast. When he awoke he found out that the other angels had saved Kaila. Now they had come to save his mother, and hopefully escape Volkhan's wrath. His mother pulled him close and held him.

"I am proud of you, my son," she said. She pulled his cap off and caressed his hair. "You are a man now. Not the kind of man that your father is, but a true man...worthy to take your place among the Wards." She spoke of the tribe of men, kinsmen to the Astrids, that he would belong to had he been born of someone that was not a hunter.

She turned to Slatkin. "I thank you for saving my son. I ask though, what must we do? How do we hide from Volkhan? He will surely track us down. He is one of the best hunters. He will find us no matter where we go...I of all people should know this. He is impossible to hide from. I have tried many times and each time I have failed." She looked to Slatkin for guidance.

"We leave before dawn," he said. "We will burn everything. The cabin and everything that belongs to you will be destroyed. We will keep only what we must take. We will bathe ourselves in the river...erase all of our scents. I can cover our tracks easily enough, but the scents and familiarities are much harder to hide. We will make our way to the Astrid tribe. Surely, they will take you back, Khali."

A deep frown lined Khali's lips and tears welled in her eyes. "I don't think they will," she said. "I am shamed now. The hunters have taken away my spirit-gift. I am a disgrace to them."

"At first it may seem so, but I think that you will find that they are forgiving...once they hear your tale. Besides, the tribe is diminishing. It would seem likely that they would accept one who knows their ways, and one who can be taught in their ways." He motioned toward Kaila, who rested with the dogs.

"What about me?" Galan asked.

"You would have to part from your mother, as all the young men in the tribe must. I will see you to the borders of your kinsmen, the Wards. They will teach you how to find your own spirit-gift."

"They will not see me as a kinsman," he said. "Volkhan is my father. I am an enemy in their eyes."

"I'm sure you will see, Galan, that not all tribes are like the hunters. They may accept you." Slatkin paused, considering the possibility. "If they do not, then you can come back with me to the king's castle. I'm sure Victor would find work for you."

"We'll worry about such things when we must. For now, let us rest," Khali said to her son. That was the sign for them all to sleep. Khali made sure that they were all comfortable then she blew out all the candles. Only the embers remained in the fire, and they glowed warm and dim as sleep came to the weary.

Kaila dreamed of her mother, but it was not what she had dreamed the previous night. Slatkin was not controlling her visions this night. She saw her mother's death over and over again in her mind. Sometimes it was clearer than others, but each time it was just as painful, if not more so than the real event. Her dreams twisted the scenes of reality, and sometimes things changed. In one scene, she was never saved, and she had died along with her mother. In another, her mother had dodged the attack from the metal beast, and had slain it. In one of the visions, Galan was killed. In another, she had thrown her knife as she ran from the cabin, and it had pierced the metal woman. She was able to kill her and save her mother...then she woke herself up crying. Upon waking, she began sobbing uncontrollably. Her whole body was shaking as she realized that she hadn't saved her. She couldn't. Her mother was still dead. The overwhelming grief struck her, crushing her from the inside. Slatkin lay awake, but he did not come to her aid. The longer he kept her from her grief, the harder it would hit her when she did finally feel it. It was best to let her mourn in the night when the others were sleeping. He knew she would be ashamed of her tears more so if the others were to see them. Now was the best time to let her shed them. Eventually she exhausted herself and fell back into a dreamless sleep.

The night was quiet, but they didn't have long to sleep. Slatkin awoke them all very early and hurried them to gather only what was necessary. "Take only the clothes on your back and whatever is sacred to you. Anything else must be left!"

Khali started to pack food, but Slatkin only let her pack a small sack for emergencies. It wasn't even enough to make a meal for one person. Galan gathered only his weapons, but was both furious and sad when he was told that he couldn't take his sled or dogs.

"If your sled is here, then Volkhan will not suspect that you have intentionally burned the cabin. Besides, they will come back to you later," Slatkin told him. He spoke to each one of the dogs and they scattered themselves into the woods. The cabin was made of Kial Thieren wood, so it burned well once ignited. It was no hard task to simply scratch a weak spot in the wood and light a candle to catch the flame to the wood. In moments, a blaze was burning high and the three travelers made their way further into the forest. Alexandria was not here to keep an eye on the cabin and control the fire, but Slatkin knew what he was doing. Part of the forest may burn...but that would make it look even more like an accident...a fire that had gotten out of hand.

The flames caught easily enough. Khali gripped her son's arms tightly. She felt both relief and sorrow as the flames quickly spread, devouring the cabin in a chaotic dance. Galan and Khali both stared at the glow of firelight as it spread. Galan felt a sobering desperation. There would be no going back to the home that he knew. He watched with his mother as the flames erased their past.

The kial thieren trees were responding to the call of the flames. The branches began creaking and reaching out to the flames, as if they were warming their hands by a hearth. Soon they were joyously burning with the cabin, and their fragrant aroma filled the forest. It was a sweet, minty odor that when accompanied by the rolling clouds of smoke, quickly masked the travelers' presence.

"We must leave now," said Slatkin. "The trees are willing to aid us if we hurry. We'll move with the smoke as far as the river. They all turned to follow the angel. Galan turned to help his mother, who he could barely see through the thick smoke, but when he turned, she was moving quickly ahead of him. She was limber and agile, like an animal that knew its way through a well-traveled path.

Kaila moved quickly beside him, but she often stopped and stared back at the flames behind them. The trees did not burn or move as normal trees would. They burned with the flames, but remained undamaged themselves. They were never burnt or harmed by the fire and they seemed to be almost dancing, reveling in the heat. Each time she looked back, though, Slatkin urged her forward.

"Our path lies toward the river, not back at the cabin," he would say to her, and Galan would reach out for her hand to pull her forward with them.

VI. The Embers of Betrayal

The hunters could smell the sweet-scented smoke drifting from the fire as soon as they crossed into the forest from the barren lands. They had traveled quickly, not stopping for rest or food. They were like the woman that had taken the lead as the party had traveled to the barren lands. Their speed surprised even them. They had not felt the desire to stop for food or rest as they raced without steeds toward their destination. Smoke hung heavy in the air. Ashes and cinders still popped, sizzled, and drifted through the air. As they got closer to his cabin, the snow-covered ground turned to black sludge. Volkhan knew what was ahead, even before he saw it. The smoke was coming from his home. He slowed his pace as he stared before him at the charred, dilapidated structure that still smoldered before him. He inhaled a deep breath of smoke-filled air, then exhaled a long, low growl. The razed timbers of kial wood that had been the frame of his cabin glowed red and hot. He kicked the one closest to him.

Sparks and ashes erupted and then disintegrated into the cold air.

"So, Malik was right," grunted Haz. "He's not here."

Volkhan stared at Haz with furrowed brows and slanted eyes. He said nothing but walked over to the remains of the charred sled. He grabbed the reins in a tight fist. Huffing with anger, he managed to speak.

"What I would like to know is if the dogs came back without him, or not. Someone unhitched them." He suspected that they came back without him. And he guessed so much more. The creature had taken the boy, but not to kill him. The boy had willingly left, he knew it, and he felt it deep within his gut. They had all escaped, they were running from him. The betrayal twisted inside of him, gnawed at his nerves, and aggravated his anger.

"How do you think the fire started?" Haz asked as he pilfered through the ashes with a hand that was half hoof, with a thumb sticking out.

Volkhan pondered for a moment. "I'm sure that it was set on purpose. I want to know why. They've betrayed me as well as the tribe…they've sided with the creature. He protects them," he surmised.

"Where do you think they went?" asked Haz. Volkhan sniffed the air. The burning kial wood was powerful and overwhelming, covering all traces of any other scent. He couldn't make out the smell of anything else. It frustrated him. Ashes were everywhere. The fire was hot and flames still erupted at times from the beams. He turned to Haz.

"See if you can find the direction that they would have taken, any tracks," he ordered.

Volkhan turned back to the cabin. He walked around the remains of the structure, searching for clues as to where his family could have gone, and how the cabin could have caught fire. The fire had been so hot that it was hard to make out what any of the remains used to be. Slick, dripping wax ran through boards, remnants of candles that had been set into fixtures along the walls. No furniture remained, just heaps of ashes with rubble strewn about. He could make out where the kitchen had once been. The chimney still stood, though the stones, instead of their natural grey, were charred black.

Then there was a change in scent. Volkhan leaned into it, the smell was enticing to him. It reminded him of his wife. It was her scent. He recognized it as the oil that she would put on her skin to protect her from the cold. He didn't know what it was, or where it came from, but it turned his thoughts to her. When he closed his eyes, he could visualize her there and he had a fierce longing to have her there suddenly. It was a yearning unlike anything he had felt before.

His memories took him back to when he had first seen her. He had been injured. It was a fall. He had lost his footing, and he had fallen several feet from a ledge. He had lain there, unable to move with a broken leg. He had thought about using his arms to crawl away, but he could not muster the strength. Each time he had moved, the pain had become more unbearable. She had been laying traps for small game when she noticed him lying close by. She did not speak his language, but she was speaking to him. Volkhan could tell from her manner that she had no harmful intentions. She had made a splint for his leg and offered him water. He didn't know what she said to him, but she said many things to him in her language that day.

Her voice had been soothing, but even more so was her scent.

It was the same smell that drew him to her on another day. It was many months later and his leg had healed. He had been hunting wolves. It was long ago, but the memory came to him sharp and clear. They had planned to hunt by the river where a large pack of wolves had been spotted. But when they got there, the wolves had vanished. Instead, a group of women were fishing by the river. The hunters had strayed into Astrid land, and they had been a tough group to catch. There was one for each of them, and Volkhan knew immediately which one he wanted to take. He recognized her face as soon as he saw her. She had been screaming at the other women, but he didn't know the language she spoke, only that she was his chosen one. Other women had cried when he took them, whimpering like animals, but she did not. She had stiffened herself to his touch and spat in his face. It amused him. He remembered that he had even fought for her. Another hunter had also spotted her when his own prize had gotten away. As Volkhan had roped her to his horse, the other hunter had blindfolded her, only to reach out to grab her. Volkhan had wrestled the other hunter into the snow, and it ended with the other one receiving a mortal wound from his hunting knife. Volkhan knew he would do it again. He would kill to have her back.

She was like no other woman. He didn't understand exactly how she was different, but there was no doubt that she was special. She had slowly learned his language, and could speak it fluently now, but even before she knew it, there seemed to be an understanding in her. She had a way of looking into his eyes and making him feel emotions that had no name in his language. It was as if she could look into him and see things that only he knew. Then, she had given birth to his son. Galan was like her, seeing things that no one else could. Volkhan was never absolutely certain, but he was convinced that they both held the gift that the hunters had sought for many years. They could see the Khanhine-lupah.

He could see her shining eyes, a deep brown color, and her long, black hair, soft to the touch. He could feel her next to him. He could feel the way she wrapped herself around him. He could hear the healing music in her voice. Suddenly, a fury came over him. He could not control it.

He wanted her here, but she had found her chance to escape. He understood it clearly now. She was gone. She had set fire to the house to escape him. She had tried before and failed. Now was his chance to find her one last time, one last time, because she was his and his alone. He had killed to get her and he would do it again.

She had left, and both the boy and the girl were with her. He had no evidence, but it must be so! He stood there pondering this. After all, the beast should have been able to kill them easily. The only other reasonable thing he could think of was that the beast was keeping them from him, luring him into a fight.

Haz called to him. "Somehow, the tracks have all been wiped. The fire has melted all the snow and exposed the tree roots. There're no traces of anyone; too many ashes and tree roots sticking up everywhere. There's nothing!"

Volkhan felt himself changing then. It was not anything he could at the moment control, but he felt it in his anger and his frustration. He screamed furiously, it sounded throughout the forest as a howl. He looked down and his hands were once again metal claws, long and sharp. He laughed then, but it erupted as a growl.

"I've got a scent!" he exclaimed. Then he ran, following the lingering smell of the oil that now hung in the air, separate from the scent of burning kial wood. Haz followed behind.

VII. A Kingdom to Build

Victor was waiting, pacing back and forth by the destroyed gate of the castle. He knew that his daughter would be returning soon. It made him anxious. Now that he had both of his lost family members back with him, it was like he was existing in a dream. He had been lost, lonely, and without power for seven years. Now all the past years had faded away, and although he could not forget them, it was hard to imagine that either reality was happening. He was somewhere in-between, able to realize them both. Having lost his family, he felt that he was able to care about them even more deeply than before.

Every time he remembered the night that he found his daughter...that first sound of her heartbeat and the musical rhythm that it beat to, his own heart leapt. He couldn't wait to see her again. Any time lost with her was too much time gone by. He paced back and forth by where the gate had once stood. He could feel her coming closer and then there she was, sitting atop her aunt's unicorn, her golden hair gleaming in the darkness. Alexandria rode atop the beast, sitting behind Angelik. Both of them approached with smiles on their faces. Alexandria wrapped in a white tiger pelt with three black-painted lines covering one eye, and Angelik with golden curls gleaming from beneath the hood of her white-fur hood. Victor felt his own smile, something that now was becoming more familiar with the return of his family. Angelik all but jumped off the unicorn into her father's waiting embrace, her arms tightening around his neck.

"Oh, you're safe!" they each said to the other in unison. Laughter followed.

"Where's mother?" she asked.

"She's inside," he responded, with a smile. He turned to Alexandria.

"Where's Slatkin?" Victor asked.

Alexandria shook her head as she dismounted. "On duty," she said. "Let's talk inside. We have a lot to tell you," she said.

Victor nodded his head in understanding. He took Angelik by her hand and led her inside, his heart leaping with glee when she looked up at him with a smile. As he walked forward with her small hand in his, he felt stronger and lighter, and he was sure that there was a spring in his step that had not been there before.

When they were inside, Carmina greeted them both with a low curtsy, though she was almost taller than them all, even in this gesture.

Victor smiled. "Carmina..." he started to say something, but then shook his head. It amused him that after all this time, she was intent upon upholding the formalities of the kingdom...and why not let her? After all, if they were to rebuild, then she could help instruct those who had forgotten. "Please stand," he said, so that she would not be holding that position until her back broke. Immediately, she perked up and followed them, pulling out the chairs for them all to sit. Alexandria gave a slight nod as she sat. Victor rushed to seat himself while she slid out a chair for Angelik.

"My king, I apologize for..." Victor just looked at her and smiled.

"Carmina," he said, looking back at her. His expression related how ridiculous he thought it all to be.

She tightened her lips. "I feel I should practice. The kingdom will be thriving soon, and I feel it is a necessity."

Victor nodded. "I hope so," he agreed, "but do not expect me to uphold any formalities until I have to. I never liked the formalities anyway."

"I know," she said. Then she looked to the door.

At that moment, Celeste walked into the room. Rolls of maps were piled in her arms. She dropped them on the table and then hurried to greet her sister and daughter. The joyous reunion went on for as long as they could allow it, but time was pressing, and there was much to do and little time to do it.

"So how did you escape that cursed land?" Alexandria asked them both.

"We couldn't have done it without Arik," said Celeste.

Victor spoke. "He took me to Kristiniva, and kept Celeste safe while I confronted her, and reclaimed Celeste's power that she had stolen. Once I did that, he brought us back home."

"Did you kill her?" she asked.

Victor just shook his head.

"I would have killed her," Alexandria said.

Victor nodded in understanding. "I thought that I would, but I couldn't. She's a goddess and the Astrids need her," he said, before asking about her adventures. "What about when you went away, where did you go and what happened to Slatkin?" Victor asked.

Alexandria sighed. "When we left, we each had a trail. Mine went cold. Her expression hardened at the memories. There were murders, but the murderer is...not human, and not guilty of her own accord. She's a creature of Shadow. Void of her own soul. She was accompanied by a band of hunters. The Shadow has corrupted them now, mostly all of them. The Shadow enticed them through their darkest emotions. I burned the corpses of Khabria and Havink and collected my power, but the time was not yet right to use it...I cannot kill the woman."

"And I saved a girl," said Angelik.

Alexandria nodded and continued. "Yes both Angelik and Slatkin had trails leading into the barren lands. Nometheog has a stronghold there. It's vast... the size of an entire city. It's constructed from a foreign material; a black metal. We followed the hunters there and both Slatkin and Angelik saved a hunter, Kaila and her brother, Galan. Slatkin is now with them. He will be gone for a long time. His intentions are to go back for Khali, Galan's mother, and take them all to the Astrids. He thinks that they'll be safe there."

Victor sighed heavily. "This is all troubling to me," he said. "The woman that you cannot kill; what power does she have over you?"

"She's metal," said Alexandria, "and she can grow weapons."

"Grow weapons?" Celeste asked.

Alexandria nodded, and they all thought about it. Alexandria knew no other way to explain what she had seen in her vision of the death of Havink and Khabria.

"There are creatures in Shea," said Celeste, "they are called selbdes. They spoke of the Shadow creatures. This woman that you cannot kill, she must be one of them. The Shadow does indeed control them, and our land is slowly being devoured by the void, by these creatures, but I've just gotten back. I will not give up hope of reclaiming this land!"

Victor took it upon himself to start unrolling the maps so that everyone could look. The largest was not just the island of Sark but a map of all the known world that stretched beyond the seas. He remembered the map fondly. He had been part of its' making. Alexandria peered curiously at it. She could see Trealon, the island of her birth, to the West and Chimrion to the South. There were many islands surrounding Sark, and far away there were large continents. There were smaller maps also; one was of the entire island of Sark. It mapped out the various tribes. Angelik could see that Sark was the largest island in a chain that could have made up its own continent. The map was outdated, though. It showed Sark as it was before she was born. She saw that there were three main tribes, the Astrids, Quinlans, and Wards. There were several towns spread throughout the island. The largest was Keru. It was the closest to the castle. Then further south was Saletu, it seemed to be built along the seaside, a port town. By the river, close to the tribe of the Quinlans was another town Ghaelrik. Bordering the barren lands was the smallest town, Viros, then another port town along the Eastern coastline, Pirikhelt. The northern forests were labeled as royal hunting lands.

Then there were maps for each of the towns. Victor pushed all of them aside except the one for Keru. "This is the only one left," he said. Celeste inhaled and exhaled slowly, feeling shock and pain at the loss. She pulled it forward.

"The hunters have taken all the other towns," she said, almost to realize it herself.

"No," said Victor. "They didn't just take them. They razed them. There's nothing left, even at Saletu," he said solemnly. "They destroyed it all. If not for Saltook's pack, they would have taken Keru as well."

Celeste swallowed hard and stared again at the maps. Then she looked seriously at Victor. "What is left of Keru?"

Victor shook his head. "Not a lot. The tavern, the stables, the farrier and blacksmith. There's a seamstress that works out of the tavern and not much else." Victor knew that it was hard for his wife to see this, but he dared not apologize. After all, he had not been able to save any of it, not even her. Treason and betrayal were the worst part of all of it. These hunters used to work for him, dine with him, he even hunted with them in his youth. They had been comrades, friends. And they all betrayed him. The skin on his face turned a dark shade of orange and he felt a searing pain as he remembered. Only this time, there were not only the usual memories, but new ones, his wife's. The way that they had beaten her and drug her bruised pregnant body through the snow…that alone was enough to make him nauseous. He sat down and shook it away as Alexandria spoke.

"There's more, to your kingdom, though. There's a new tribe, one made up of the children that you took into the castle. The Schithronians. That is what they call themselves. They are loyal to you and they fight against the hunters."

Celeste's eyes lit up, "They survived?" she asked, astonished.

"Yes. I have been to their den. They survive in tunnels beneath", she looked at the map for reference "Ghaelrik…or at least what it used to be. There's a dense forest there now."

Celeste nodded. "I must visit them!" She exclaimed.

"And there are others that will come to your aid," she said. "I will journey back to Chimrion. They will ally with you and come here to aid you, I know it. There are good people there, great warriors and wizards. They can help us."

She looked then to Celeste. "I know that you don't want me to make the suggestion because it is still so close to your personal experience, but you must go to the elves. I know that they are part of the land that stole you from us, but you know that this is their chosen home. They want you here and they will help you, no matter the cost." Alexandria pointed to the spot on the map where they would be. "There, that is where you'll find them. Wouldn't you say so, Victor?"

He nodded then turned to his wife. "She's right, Celeste. They will be some of our most powerful aid. After all, I'll have to admit that I would never have found you if not for Arik guiding me there."

She gave a reluctant nod. "I'll include them, though I'm sure that I already owe Arik more than I can ever repay him."

Victor turned his attention from the map to his wife. "Well, Celeste, how do you want to do this?"

She studied it with him. "Alexandria will go to Chimrion. The rest of us will go together. We will visit the tavern at Keru first, then take the quickest road to the Scithronians, and then we will visit the elves on our way back."

"Shouldn't you split into two groups?" reasoned Alexandria. "You will get the job done faster."

"No," said Celeste. "No, not unless it is a necessity. We've waited too long to be together just to part again."

Victor smiled. He nodded as he looked to his sister-in-law. "Not unless we have to. That I can promise!"

"So when do we leave?" Alexandria asked.

"When will you be ready?" Victor asked.

"If I can get a few days' worth of supplies, I can be on my way tonight."

"My mind is already made up," said Celeste. "We will leave tonight. Time is against us and the Shadow edges closer as we speak. We must gather all those loyal to us and bring them back here, to the castle. It is the best that we can do for them."

VIII. River Crossing

The four travelers ran through the forest with smoke masking their bodies, hiding their escape. They reached the river and stared out into the expanse of blackness before them. All the stars in the sky were mirrored in the sleek blackness of the river's ice.

"You must not be afraid if the ice gives way," said Slatkin.

Khali knelt before the river, running her hand smoothly over the ice. The beads on her bracelet glowed faintly, each one a different color. "The gods are with us," she said confidently.

"It's a long way," said Kaila as she gazed across the starlit expanse.

"Can you make it?" Galan asked his sister. She shrugged.

"I'll carry you if you can't. It's either this way or die. Volkhan will be going to that cabin before he searches anywhere else."

Kaila sighed and nodded her head.

Slatkin smiled and stepped out onto the ice. Only a slight tingle could now be felt in his bare feet. He peered into the distance. A faint orange glow could be seen on the Eastern shore of the river. "Stay with me and do not be afraid. Saigolai aids us."

Khali stepped out after him. Her boots were thick and made to withstand instances such as these. She pressed forward, and then turned back to the children. Galan was on the ice, the spikes on the bottom of his shoes helped to steady him, but Kaila was reluctantly stepping forward. She walked only a few steps before she slipped. Galan reached out to catch her and helped her to stand. He knelt down. "Here," he said, "I'll carry you." He quickly hoisted his sister on to his back and they continued forward.

Millions of stars dotted the sky. The reflection of the stars on the black ice was both breathtaking and disorienting. It was as if the sky had fallen, and they were carefully stepping through the cosmos. Both below and above, twinkling stars winked with the protection of the gods. It was a long journey. Hardly any words crossed between them. Their efforts went into carefully plotting where to put down their foot next and concentrating on staying upright. Kaila was concerned that Galan would drop her but whenever she felt herself slipping, he would hoist her up higher and continue. Slatkin was always aware of where the others were stepping. He knew that the ice would give way; it was just a question of how far they could travel before having to face that obstacle. He didn't worry, though. His father was looking out for them. That he knew. Many other things were not yet revealed to him, but he knew enough to continue to guide them forward over the treacherous ice, leading them slowly towards a light that seemed no closer than when they began the dangerous trek. Galan looked back, but could not see the place where they started. It was as if they were not moving now, just suspended in the sky, floating with no beginning to go back to and no end. Then as if Saigolai was presenting them with guidance, colors began to sweep through the sky to light their way. At first in green, then reds and blues followed. Khali held up her bracelet. The stones lit up brighter.

"A gift of light!" she exclaimed.

Slatkin smiled. "Yes," he said, "we'll need it soon. The ice is getting thin."

The others looked down. The ice was wet here. Water was sinking into their boots. "Remember," Slatkin said. "Do not be afraid if the ice gives way."

They pressed on carefully, slowly. Then there was an earsplitting crack close by, but the ice did not give way this time. Khali reached out to her son.

"Saigolai is with us," she said. Then she reached out to Kaila. "Do not forget that," she told her. The child's eyes were bright with fear.

"I'm not a good swimmer!" Kaila whispered.

"The gods will know this. Do not be afraid."

They stepped forward, surrounded by the dancing colors of the aurora borealis, then another earsplitting crack followed by an enormous splash. Galan struggled to hold to his sister and still swim. Her scream was muffled by the splashing. She kicked her feet, but continued to sink. Galan swam towards her. It was too cold to scream the words that he was thinking. He went under the water to grab her. They struggled for a moment. He grabbed her and resurfaced. Her sudden coughing and gasping for air sent relief through him. She was alive. While he had been saving her he had been unconcerned with their surroundings and was himself alarmed when he realized he was being lifted out of the water. His shaking sister was still clutched numbly in his arms and they were being lifted onto a boat by Slatkin. Khali was removing her clothes and dumping them into the river. Galan was shivering uncontrollably, his teeth chattering.

"It is alright, you can let her go," said Slatkin. The cold was so deep that Galan couldn't feel himself releasing her. "Do as your mother is doing. We must throw our clothes and furs to the river. Volkhan cannot trace us as easily if we lose them. There are replacement clothes there, on the shore. Until then, we have blankets to wrap ourselves in. Galan couldn't feel anything. Every movement was full of piercing, cold pain. He had to watch every motion that he made to make sure that he was indeed moving. He could feel nothing, especially in his fingertips. It was a task, but they were soon undressed and wrapped in blankets. That's when he noticed someone rowing the boat. He couldn't make out their facial features. The lights had vanished from the sky, and all was darkness again. They soon reached the shore. There was a fire lit at the edge of the shore. Several figures sat around it. There was a smell of cooking food. His stomach rumbled when he inhaled the aroma. As they reached the fire, he recognized that the person who was rowing the boat was a young woman with a tangled mass of black hair.

"We brought food, furs, and clothes, just as Klarissa asked us to."

"Thank you," said Slatkin. "This is Khali, Galan, and Kaila," Slatkin said, pointing to the other three. "I am Slatkin."

"You we know!" the woman said. "I never thought I would save hunters, though!" she exclaimed, "Even if Saigolai *did* will it."

"A lot is changing," said Slatkin.

She nodded. "I know," she said. "Come," she offered. "These clothes should be warm and dry. Sit and eat!" she offered. "I'm Valassa!" She looked down at the hunters. "We are the Scithronians." Another from her group gave them all clothes to change into. With painfully numb fingers, Galan dressed himself in the new clothes woven of kial fabric. There was also a coat and boots made of a rare grey fur. He gave it an approving look, and then sat close to the fire. The warmth spread itself through his freezing bones. He felt tired, but before he could sleep, someone handed him a bowl of soup and a mug of hot, spiced drink. "Eat. Your strength will come back soon."

Galan looked over at his sister. She was dressed in the same rare colored fur and she had been given a bowl as well, but she did not eat. Her lips held a blue tint, and her skin was an unusual color, even close to the fire, she did not look healthy. Her eyes were closing. He reached out a hand to shake her.

"Wake up!" he exclaimed.

"I'm tired," she whispered.

"Eat now and you can sleep later," he said, while his teeth chattered uncontrollably. "Please," he said, "please don't sleep yet." Her hands were wrapped in mittens, but her body still shivered. Galan placed the bowl to her lips. "Here, Kaila."

She slowly sipped the spiced drink and the color of her lips gradually changed from blue tinted to a healthy pink. His mother ate her soup, not talking. She watched the children interact with a smile on her face. She had raised him right. Her heart swelled with joy. He may have been born to a hunter, but he was a Ward. Slatkin hastily ate his soup and then fell into a conversation with their rescuer. They walked a distance from the campfire. Galan could hardly make out their words, but there were a few sentences that he overheard.

"If not for her visions, we may very well have failed," Slatkin said, with his smooth, deep voice. "I thank you. I know how hard it is for you to save a hunter, but I saved Galan. He is a hunter no more! I can promise you."

"According to Klarrissa, he never has been a hunter like the rest of them. He is special. His gift is hidden to him, but one day, he will see it."

There was silence for a while then Galan heard his sister's name. "Kaila is a hunter at heart, but she is not evil. Her mother and Havink have taught her good things. They were not evil, and that is why the Shadow destroyed them. He is eliminating all who do not follow him. If not for Galan, she would be dead. He kept her alive until Angelik could get there."

"Klarissa is willing to help him. There are more gods protecting him than just the god of life. Not all of them with pure intentions. His spirit-gift is strong. She could help him unlock his gift.

"No. His gift belongs with his kin. We will seek out the Astrids and Wards. They can teach him to use it for good in the world. If they deny him, then I will reconsider."

"You risk leaving him to the Quinlans and Hunters. They would enslave him, and use his gift for evil purposes."

"I understand that. His father saw it. He knew that he had the gift. That's why he was allowed to live with him. That is why his mother was not killed. Volkhan did what the hunters have been trying to do for many years. Galan doesn't understand it all, but he will in time."

Galan turned to his sister. She was wiping the tears from her eyes with the back of her hand. It alarmed him. "What's wrong Kaila?" he asked her. At first, she did not speak, then very faintly, she whispered. "I lost my dagger in the water." She looked at him then, her gaze was lost and far away. "My mother made it for me. It was carved from Valka bone." Galan nodded his head. "I will get it back for you. I promise. Rest here." he patted her back gently then stood to make his way to the boat, but one of the Scithronians stopped him. "Where are you going?" The man's voice came out as a growl.

"My sister lost her Valka blade. I have to get it back for her."

The man laughed. "We got your weapons. Don't worry about it. Rest!"

"Let me see, then." Distrust was dominant in his tone. "She'll never sleep without her blade."

The man nodded his head, and walked with Galan to the boat. Inside was a sack, and sure enough, within the bag were all of their weapons. He searched out Kaila's blade, and his own hunting knife, just in case he needed it.

"No need for that tonight," the man said. "There is plenty to eat."

"It's not for food. It's just in case...I'm not sure how far away Volkhan is, but I, like my sister, will not sleep without my blade. Just in case he finds me while I rest."

The Scithronian nodded his head. "Take them all then, if you need them."

Galan shook his head, "Just this one while I sleep."

They walked back to the fire and Galan placed the Valka blade into his sister's lap. Her eyes lit up when she saw it. She turned to her brother and nodded her head. "Thank you," she said.

Galan smiled. "I knew that I better get it back for you. After all, I need someone to stand watch while I sleep in case Volkhan comes for me."

Her eyes widened. She frowned, then smiled a little as she realized that he was teasing. But then the thought became a possibility in her mind and she looked at him seriously.

"Do you think that he will?" she asked. Galan shrugged, smiling a little. He had meant to tease her, but the reality of the idea sank in to him as well.

"I don't know. I hope not."

Kaila's lips quivered, she stared down at the blade, gripping it firmly. A dark fire burned in her eyes as she looked at it, then she turned to Galan. "I want you to teach me how to kill Volkhan." Galan just looked at her for a moment. His expression turned complicated.

"No. I can't teach you that." He paused and sighed. "Anyway, I don't know how. But I can teach you how to survive if he comes to kill you." Galan's mouth quivered a little as he spoke to his sister. A dark expression fell over him. "If I could kill him, then I would have already done it, many years ago. I have wanted to kill Volkhan many times but it is not as easy as it seems. He hurts my mother, and there have been many times that I thought she would die." His eyes stung as he spoke. "And sometimes I thought that I would die. But no matter how much he hurt me, or my mother, I couldn't do it. He is my father. Something about it seems wrong…besides, our father is strong, and fast, and smart. There is a reason he was chosen as a leader. He is not easy to kill."

"Teach me whatever you know," she said.

"I will teach you. I promise, Kaila." She managed a weak smile and nodded her head with acceptance. With those words said, the two children lay down to rest for the night, guarded by Slatkin and the Scithronians.

IX: Malik

Malik ran quickly to the river. There were many scents that were now appealing to him. Some were more animal, others were human. The river was breaking up; sheets of ice moved swiftly across its expanse. He followed it to the ford. It was only as deep as his waist here. He dove in and quickly swam across, the coldness never bothering him. When he emerged on the other side of the river, he knew that he was close to the boy and the girl, but there were other smells now that enticed him. Some were close, some were farther, but each of them tickled his appetite.

He slowed his pace, stepping through the cold snow, carefully trying to target just one of the scents that wafted around him. He decided on a sweet one. It was warm, and he could tell it would be filling to him. He sniffed the air, and quietly moved forward. Time seemed to slow as he used all of his efforts to try to subdue the buzzing in his throat that became louder with his excitement. He edged through the forest. There were animals creeping by him. He was hyper aware of their movements, their heartbeats, and the flow of blood racing through their veins. The sweet smell was close now. Adrenaline surged through him. The creature came closer.

A man. He was simply walking, nothing more. For some reason, his blood seemed tastier than anything else he had sniffed. Instinctively, Malik raised his hand. A needle shot from his fingertip. The man grabbed his arm, staring around. Malik watched the man with interest. He could see darkness already swelling in the wound. Soon there were dark traces of his venom tracing their way through the man's veins. The man fell down, obviously in pain. Malik walked slowly forward, unable to stall his hunger any longer. Another needle slipped from his hand, and he aimed it for the man's neck. It hit. Attached to the second needle was a tube. The man's blood slowly crawled through the tube. Malik smiled with intrigue at his new weapons. The man just stared at him. A mix of confusion and maddening agony filled his face but he was unable to fight back and could only watch as his own blood slowly left his body and filtered into Malik. Malik laughed. It was a strange, but wonderful sensation. The blood was warm, and it tasted just as sweet as it smelled. Yet, how he could taste it, he was unsure. When he had extracted his fill, the needle attached to the tube retracted back into his fingertip. He watched then as the black poison spread throughout the man, his skin turning paler until he was a white, cold, hardened shell, striated with black poison.

Malik was full now, but the smells and movements of the forest were all the more enticing to him. He moved forward. There were more men like this one. He would be hungry again soon and the voice had spoken to him earlier. *Eat to your belly's content. Fill yourself with lively blood. Just answer me when I call for you.* That was his purpose and intent for the moment, to eat to his belly's content.

X. Memories

Carmina had readied four steeds, two black stallions, one white unicorn and one grey mare. Victor and Celeste sat atop the two black with Angelik in front of her mother, and Carmina rode atop the gray. Alexandria rode atop Vortex, her unicorn. They traveled forward towards the tavern. There was a warming breeze blowing; never a good sign in a Sarkian winter.

The women rode in front, talking about things they missed, and things that they wanted to accomplish. Victor rode behind them, drifting off into memories that were not his.

Celeste stared at a face through the flames. Long, black hair, one blue eye, and one blind, white eye stared back from a face that was still healing, clawed by a bear. The one man who had led the others in the raid on the castle...Darkhan stared back at her with a look of malicious rage. The torch that had set the fire still burned brightly in his bandaged hand. Victor concentrated on the face, even though he could feel the flames, the same flames that were consuming his wife. He could feel the contractions as the child inside sought a safer world. Lashes from whips cracked against his skin, giving the flames a new way to burn. All the while, Darkhan smiled, relishing the pain. Celeste had cried out for him, for Victor, but he was across the sea, called out to a war that never happened.

"Victor?" He came back from the memory, still atop his horse, still moving forward, but they were at the tavern and it was time to stop now. His body went through the motions of tying his horse to the post, but he was lost in these memories, this pain of his wife's suffering.

Suddenly, she was there before him, her hand resting on his cheek. "Victor," she said. He closed his eyes and reached up to rest his hand with hers.

"Celeste," he said. "Never listen to anyone who tries to tell you that you are weak," he said.

"What?" she asked.

"I'm sorry," he said, steeling himself against the emotions and memories that he could not rid himself of. There was so much more that he wanted to say, but how could you put any of what she had felt that night into words, and how could he fit all the things that he was sorry for into just one 'I'm sorry'?

"Victor," she said. "Stop apologizing!" she said. She knew what he was feeling. She knew that he was reliving her memories. "I have never blamed you for any of it," she said.

He nodded, opening his eyes, while blinking away the stinging wetness that clung there. "I know, Celeste, but *I* do. *I* blame *myself*. I should have been there! You called my name out...but I never came."

She shook her head. "Yes," she admitted, "but I wasn't calling your name for you to save me, and you know it."

"I know, Celeste. I feel it all, everything, but your feelings cannot change my own. I will carry this guilt in me forever."

She shook her head. "No, Victor. You'll see. Everything was for a reason."

He wanted to protest, to proclaim again and again his regret to her, but he knew that she would turn a deaf ear and continue to console him. It made him angry in a way. He was angry that he felt this pain and she was here for him. She had felt it alone, when there was no hope for a better tomorrow; no hope of seeing those that she loved. He wanted to be alone now as much as he wanted to be with her. It could only be fair if he experienced this away from her, away from everyone that he loved...the same as she had.

They had barely entered the door when she turned to him, hands on her hips and a reproving look on her face. "Victor!" She exclaimed in a tight-lipped whisper. "I've had enough of you punishing yourself for my feelings," she said, clearly seeing his emotions. "You went through the same loneliness that I did. You missed seven years of your daughter growing up...I want happiness. And I know that you are completely caught up in my past right now. I understand that, but you need to focus on our plan. We have to rebuild this kingdom, and my justice will come when I know that our subjects are safe from the rule of hatred that they have been under for seven years..." she stopped her rant when Alexandria's hand touched her shoulder.

"There's someone you two need to see," she said, motioning toward Saltook, the barkeep. He was an ageing man with a black and white beard and mustache, and shaggy hair of the same color. He was large and muscular. He wore an apron over his simple clothes and held a smoking kial twig between his fingers. Normally, he could be seen standing behind the bar, or scurrying around the tavern to see to the needs of his many guests. Tonight though, he left the work to his many laborers and instead of standing behind the bar, he was sitting at a table with Angelik. He was smiling and laughing jovially, as was the bright angel. There were not many people in the tavern at the moment. Many of them had already sauntered up to their rooms for the night or meandered home, drunk on multiple flasks of kial brew. The barmaids were still cleaning up tables and there were a couple of tables filled with patrons who were all but passed out, the wenches at their side looking rather bored. One of them was slipping her hand into her customer's pocket, searching for the funds that she was sure to be shorted on later. Victor caught her eye, and she quickly showed her hands, clearly free of money and pushed back her chair, motioning to her cohort. They quickly left the men at the tables, who mumbled words incoherently as the women walked away.

The three angels then came to sit at the table with Saltook, Carmina and Angelik. Saltook's eyes lit up at seeing them. He stood and bowed respectfully. Angelik giggled as he did so. She was still not used to the formalities. Victor was still too caught up in the memories to even say anything about the formality. It was Celeste who spoke.

"Please, Saltook, there's no need for the formality right now. We mean to sit and have a conversation with you. Please join us." Saltook seated himself as he had been asked.

"My queen, I...I'm speechless, where have you been?"

"Trapped. Imprisoned. Enslaved by a goddess that is not my own."

"You should know that we have grieved for you. Your absence has filled us all with unbearable sorrow! My heart feels immense joy at your return."

"Your words are felt, Saltook, and I thank you for your loyalty. I too, have missed all of my subjects."

Alexandria spoke next. "Saltook, if ever there was a time to claim your loyalty, it is now. The land of Sark, as you know, has been overrun with evil but as frightening as it may sound, the hunters are the least of our worries. A much larger threat is building in the barren lands, east of here."

Saltook shook his head. "What could be worse than those…sadistic, feral…evil men?"

"A god that has secretly crept into their beliefs. Nometheog. The Shadow god of the void. They have long ago forgotten the beliefs of Khanhine, as you well know," said Celeste.

"Aye! That they have! It's sacrilege, what they do!" His voice was raised and he beat his fist on the table as he said it. "I will never believe that they act on Khanhine's orders."

"It's because they don't, and they haven't for years. Nometheog controls them now and his plans to secure his rein are only just beginning." said Alexandria. "I have been to the barren lands, and I have seen with my own eyes his dark city and the creatures that he has already twisted to his will. He plans to twist all the hunters into these creatures and reign with terror but as you well know, we cannot let that happen. We are asking you to aid us,

Saltook. You are faithful to both Saigolai and the true Khanhine."

Saltook nodded. "That I am, and I'm not about to change for some imposter god!"

"That is good," said Celeste with her smooth voice. "I have been away, as you know for many years, but I am back, and I can wield a powerful weapon, but I cannot do it alone. I want to know that you will be there when we need you and that you will give aid when it is needed."

Saltook nodded. "Of course, my lady. You can always count on my pack. We'll not ever let you down."

She nodded. "I know that, Saltook but it is always good to hear it from your voice and I thank you. For now, I need you to open up the tavern to all that seek safety and seek out those who are true to Khanhine, an ally of Saigolai."

"I will see to it personally, your highness!" he exclaimed, with a look of excitement and determination in his eyes. "It is, as always, an honor to serve you and the powers of life."

"Now that that's taken care of," began Alexandria. "We could use something to eat if you have any rations left from the night."

Saltook laughed. "There's always rations, here!" he exclaimed. "Basilla!" he called to his daughter, a young woman with dark hair and a rosy complexion. "Bring some of the deer roast out for our guests!" he exclaimed. Basilla smiled brightly as she curtsied, aiming her gaze at Alexandria, who had recently saved her from death at the hands of hunters.

While they waited, Victor leaned in to Saltook. "Do you have a bottle of kial brew?" he asked,

"Yes, of course," he said, then yelled at Basilla to bring a bottle of kial brew.

"Thank you, my friend," he said. He then looked around at the entrances. "Would you let Alexandria remove the enchantments, if I could promise that it would save you all?"

Both Alexandria and Saltook looked at him in shock.

"No disloyalty meant, my king, but that's been a true blessing here."

He turned to Alexandria and laughed a hearty laugh. "You should have seen some of them trying to get through that door! They were begging and pleading with all manner of excuses to get in here. Nothing that came out of their mouth was honest! Ha Ha!" He chuckled heartily. "Some of the girls were standing just out of reach inside the doors." He chuckled again. "The taunting and threats were rough on both sides, but the girls knew where the boundary was. Those boys wouldn't give up even after they got knocked on their back several times."

Alexandria chuckled along with him. She knew her own enchantments and what they could do.

"I know that I'm asking a lot, Saltook. I need you to trust me," pleaded Victor.

Just then, Basilla came with their food. Another young girl assisted her. Victor reached for the kial brew and gulped a swallow then pulled a utility knife from his boot and pricked his finger, letting the blood slide into the bottle.

"What are you doing, Daddy?" Angelik asked, wide eyed.

"I'm enacting a plan." He smiled cunningly and turned to Saltook. "Before we leave, Alexandria will remove the enchantments. As the hunters come to you, make sure they drink this, but only the hunters. You will see. They will not be a bother for long."

Saltook nodded. "I'll do it!" he agreed.

"Good," Victor said with a smile.

"So, how have the Scithronians been doing?" Alexandria asked.

Saltook smiled. "Well, to be a bunch of thieving children, they've actually been very loyal. Nothing's missing, and they all have manners, where it counts anyway," he said, chuckling to himself.

Celeste smiled, placing her hand over her heart. It made her glad to know that some of her teachings had paid off.

"Are they still here?" asked Alexandria.

Saltook nodded. "The ones that are here now have gone to rest for the night. Unless you go wake 'em, you'll have to wait until tomorrow night to speak to them."

"No, that's okay," said Celeste. "We will go speak to the rest of them in their den."

Saltook nodded. "Time is against you, I know," he said.

Celeste finished her food, then looked to Saltook. "Thank you for the meal," she said, "and for keeping the town safe when the hunters attacked."

A dark look came into Saltook's expression. "I did what I could, but I would hardly say that I kept it safe. Many died that night. Most died, in fact. I was able to fight, but the hunters had gained a power, a strength, that night that made them harder to defeat. We managed to keep the tavern, the stables. The blacksmith and farrier were able to hold their own, with a stockpile of weapons at their disposal. The seamstress fled her shop and ran here for safety. Good thing, too! The whole town went up in flames. Her shop burned as well as her own home. After the fires, there were floods.

Saltook shook his head, shaking away the memories. "The floods were worse than the fires. The weather goddess was behind that, she had to be! The winds and the rains put the fires out, but many more lost their lives to the floods. Then, when news spread of the betrayal; the raid on the castle, I was heartbroken. Like I said, I did what I could, but we lost everything."

Celeste shook her head. "No, Saltook, Victor told me of your valor. We would not have what is left of this island if you had not been here to stand up to the hunters."

XI. The Astrid Lands

"Galan," Kaila's whisper tickled his ear. Her small hand lay on his chest from attempting to shake him awake. It took him a moment to remember where he was and to realize that something was wrong. The fire had been doused, and there was movement nearby. Kaila clutched her Valka blade in her hand and stared back towards the river. He started to ask her what was wrong, but she turned to him and put a finger over her lips. She silently motioned for him to arm himself. He grabbed his hunting knife from its sheath. None of the Scithronians were nearby anymore. He assumed that was the movement that he had heard. They had been moving out into the forest. He saw no sign of his mother or the old man. He listened, but the night was silent. Millions of stars dotted the sky above the river, but he saw nothing unusual, nor was there anything else out of the ordinary. After a few moments, his mother returned. She was putting two hatchets in holders at her hips. Slatkin came back with his axe now slung in a proper holder on his back that matched the new furs he wore. Slowly the other

Scithronians appeared, all putting away weapons that they had readied before.

"What's happening?" Galan asked.

"They know you are alive, but they are not crossing the river. They are close behind us, so we must leave now before they have a chance to cross."

"Who else?" Galan asked. He assumed his father was one of the ones mentioned.

Slatkin shook his head. "I do not know," said Slatkin. "He is hard to read, like he has been altered. Your father, I sense him very faintly. I do not know who the other is, but he knows you. I can tell."

Galan felt his breathing become heavier in his chest. He stood to look at his mother and then he looked back at Slatkin. "What do you mean by altered?"

Slatkin shook his head. "I can't explain it," he said, wrinkling his brow. "He will not be the father that you once knew. He is just a remnant of the hunter Volkhan. Even I do not understand what exactly has happened to him. I can only guess."

"Well, we better move forward quickly!" exclaimed Valassa. She and Barrett had already loaded pack horses with supplies. "We'll be close behind you," she said. Slatkin took the lead and the three exiled hunters fell in between them, walking forward through drifts of snow, into the darkened forest. Galan did not see where the other Scithronians had gone, but he felt that they were not far away. They moved silently around the hunters, protecting them from all sides.

As daylight brightened the scenery around them, Galan realized that they were wearing furs with a silver sheen so that they looked white sometimes, grey at others, and in darkness they appeared black. He tried to think of what creature would have this fur, but he could not, and he didn't want to ask. He felt that it would make him seem unskilled and dumb. After all, any good hunter knew all the animals and their ways.

They traveled carefully; always looking to Slatkin whenever they heard a noise. They stopped after a few hours when the old man turned to them. "Let us stop here and rest," he said, "we'll eat and then continue forward."

Valassa and Barrett began passing out rations to the hunters. Not long after, they were resting among the roots of the kial thieren trees and eating bits of dried meat and biscuits. Galan was famished and did not even taste the food as he ate it. There was more of the spiced drink, though it was cold this time. Galan looked at his sister who ate with only one hand. The other was gripping her blade firmly. He thought back then, to the day that he had saved her life. He wanted to say something to her, but what could he say? He wished that there was a way to fix it all, but he knew that there wasn't. Saving her life was as close as he could come to correcting the wrong doing. Even as he thought it, another thought came to him: the unusual woman and the black-eyed man…what if they were aiding his father? The thought sent chills through him. He was scared enough of his father, but if they also saw him as a betrayer, then he didn't stand a chance at living. He had been lucky before, but he didn't think that he would be so lucky again. He looked at Slatkin, who seemed to always know much more than he ever told.

After they had eaten and rested, Slatkin urged them forward. "We've much farther to go," he said. "We're only half-way up the mountain; we must go down the other side before we reach our destination." So, they continued forward as they had before. When Galan could hold it in no more, he started to ask questions.

"They are with him, aren't they, the man and woman?"

"Do not worry. It is not them. Though, there are others that are formidable enough."

Galan felt that Slatkin was keeping things from him, but he did not press the issue. He felt that he could trust him. If he were keeping secrets, then Galan was sure that he had his reasons for doing so.

They traveled throughout the day, camped for the night, and continued the following morning without incident. They kept a steady speed, and they reached the Astrid lands at about midday the following day. Galan knew that they were in Astrid territory as soon as he saw the bones hanging from trees. The Astrids hollowed out wood and animal bones and hung them from the trees. His mother had explained that this was how they listened to the gods. They were placed in a special way, to ward off evil, and bring healing music into the village. He had never been to the village, only to the outskirts. The music that he heard was not pleasant. It was a lonely. low howl; like a cold wind. He felt his mother take his hand. Tears were welling in her eyes.

"I need your strength," she said to him. "I have longed to see my home, but I'm afraid that it will not be as I remember it. I'm afraid that they will not take me back…and then where will I go?"

"You'll go with me," he said. She smiled at him and nodded. Galan noticed now that the Scithronians were no longer following them. He liked to think that they had hidden themselves in the trees, and were still helping to look out for them, but he could see no one when he looked into the tangled boughs. Kaila looked up at the chimes with wonder. She had probably not ventured this far before, never having gained a title as hunter yet.

Slatkin looked at them with concern. "Galan and Kaila, they will see us only as hunters, enemies. You must trust me, though. I promise you that you will be safe with me no matter what happens. They walked forward to the edge of a wooden bridge that carried them over a deep ravine.

"Perhaps you and your son should go first, Khali," said Slatkin. Khali nodded her head and held up her bracelet with the stones. Only one stone glowed. It represented Saigolai. She moved forward, still holding to Galan's hand.

As they neared the edge of the bridge, a woman called out in the Astrid language, "You dare to tread on our holy ground? You stink of hunters!" Galan was caught off guard when he was hit forcefully in the eye with a stone. He reached up to grab his eye, and before he knew it, there was an arrow embedded in his leg. He lost his balance and fell from the bridge. For a brief moment he waded into confusion. He should have still been falling, but he was encircled in a cage made of bone, dangling over the ravine. It took him a moment to recover from his shock. He grabbed his leg near the shaft of the arrow. Blood seeped through his clothes and furs. He wanted to yell out, but the pain was so fierce that it stole his voice. He saw Kaila struggling with a large tall woman. Her screams were quickly subdued with a blow dart which pierced her left arm. She quickly slowed, obviously drugged by something on the dart. The woman was quick to bind the child's hands. His mother gave no struggle, but simply surrendered to their attackers. She was being bound at the wrists with leather straps and blindfolded. Only Slatkin remained standing upon the bridge, and he had several spears pointing at his throat.

The woman that stood before him was tall and fierce. She was dressed in simple, leather clothes. She had moccasin boots and a mask decorated with dried mud and kial thieren leaves. It resembled a kraelvin. The other women wore masks that represented other animals. Their skin was smooth and dark like Khali's and their long black hair had been caked in mud and styled to stand out from their faces so that they appeared to have crowns of spikes standing out from their heads, resembling feathers and fur.

"You are not a hunter. Why do you travel with such company?" one of the women asked him.

"Please allow us to see The Mother. If you inspect these prisoners, you will see that you have bound one of your own. The others may seem to be hunters, but I assure you that they are no longer a threat to you. We seek refuge here and healing. That is all. We come in peace."

Each woman had different pieces of jewelry which glowed when they were close to the orostiro. The one who was their leader considered this for a moment and then she motioned for the others to release their spears. Slowly, Galan's cage was hauled back onto the bridge and he was helped out. Khali was in tears, feeling the pain of what she had known would happen. They did not recognize or accept her here anymore.

Their leader had the prisoners blindfolded and their hands bound. She explained that it was to ensure their safety. If they were honest, then they would comply; if they were not, then they would be caged again. Kaila started to protest, but Slatkin intervened yet again.

"She is just a young girl," he said. "Please be soft on her hands. As you can see, she has been tied before. The hunters did not treat her well." The guard looked at the scars on her wrists and nodded.

"I see them," she said. Then instead of tying the girl's hands, she tied the rope around Kaila's waist and then tied it around her own wrist and guided the child instead of forcing her forward.

They moved forward then, as prisoners of the Astrids.

XII. Belle's Elixer

Belle leaned down to Evingh's bed and shook him gently. "Wake up, dear. It's time that you get up and have your breakfast," she said. Her voice was motherly, a soft voice that a parent used when waking a baby. The only motion that he made to show that he was awake was the fluttering of eyelashes as he opened his eyes, which stared before him. He seemed to stare past everything, into some realm, some space beyond anything that was around him. He was never aware.

"You must get out of bed," she encouraged. "I will help you if I must but you can do this."

Evingh blinked for a few seconds then he sat up. She helped him position his feet to the edge of the bed then he stood up. He stood slowly. His motions were stiff, almost as if he were being controlled by some other force. It had been like this since he had been in her care. He was once the hunter Chase, but she had renamed him. She had not known him before he was like this. She caught herself imagining what he would have been like. Part of her wanted to imagine him as a boy who was good, someone compassionate and hard-working. But she knew that was wrong. It was a fantasy of her mind's making and it had no place in reality. He was only a boy to her, but he was a man in the tribe of the hunters. A man capable of not only good, but evil. What exactly Slatkin had done to him, Belle did not know, nor could she ever fully understand, but Slatkin could only have given him a punishment that he deserved. As the hunter Chase, she did not know the damage he had done to others, but she was determined not to let him repeat his mistakes as the boy Evingh. Slatkin had entrusted her to teach him what was good. She was determined not to fail. She could not live with herself if she disappointed Slatkin.

Each night, she had awakened him as she did this day. Each night she hoped that he would improve, hoped that he showed signs of knowing...of knowing anything at all. He was always the same, though. Blank. Expressionless. She had, at times, been able to extract something reminiscent of a smile, such as when Carmina would play music, or when Belle read some small part of a story that he liked. It was these times that he would smile. Otherwise, there was nothing that she could do to get an emotion from him. Every once in a while, another expression would present itself. It was dark, almost frightened. Was he remembering something? Celeste had said that he was living in a nightmare of his own making. Was it in these times that he was at some particularly terrible part of a dream? More importantly, was there anything that Belle could do to help him, to comfort him? She did not know.

Slatkin had left her in charge of him, but he did not give any specific instructions. At times this made her furious. How could she, a mere mortal, do the job appointed to the mightiest of Saigolai's heroes?

She would get angry, but then she felt honored. Slatkin loved her, she knew it. He would never make her do something that she was not capable of. He would never burden her with something that was too much for her. She knew that if he needed her for this task, then there was a reason. She remembered clearly that he had told her that she had something within her that the boy needed, something that he could not give to him. Whatever talent lay inside of her was the only thing that could bring him back to the world.

She had helped him into his clothes and fed him his breakfast, often this task in itself was enough to make her feel tired. As the days went by, it became tiring to her to care for him. She felt lonelier than ever. Slatkin was not here and her friends had all left. It was just her and Evingh. There was no one here to ask for help or to even talk to other than him.

The winter had covered the land with snow so deep that it was difficult for her to maneuver around outside. There were tasks that she had to do each morning. There was water to draw from the well, the fires she had to build and tend to. She had to gather ingredients for cooking and then put the water on to boil. Then there were the preparations for cooking, the cooking itself. Then there was always the clean-up. All the while, Evingh was the only one there and just waking him, and dressing him gave her out before the day had even started.

She was unsure of herself, of her abilities, but she knew that she had to see this task through, no matter how hard. She had to do it for this boy, who deserved a better life, and for Slatkin. She would do anything for Slatkin.

She took the boy by the hand now, after breakfast, and smiled at him. "What would you like to do today?" she asked. She knew he would not answer, but she always presented the question. She always hoped that there would be an answer. Her question was answered with a blank stare. Belle sat in thought.

"How about we read another story? You would like that wouldn't you, Evingh?" She said his name as often as she could, hoping that it would be ingrained in him so much so that if he ever did come to, he would know to leave the name of Chase behind him.

The night followed as usual, and as Dawn broke through the darkness of night, Belle knew that it was time for rest. She had seen that Evingh was in his bed, she hoped sleeping soundly, though she was never sure. The kitchens were clean and ready for the next morning, and her body was tired. There was not a part of her that did not ache. She made her way to her comfort spot, the place where she felt most at peace. She sat by the dim firelight in the kitchens and opened up an ancient cookbook. It had been handed down to her from a witch who had taught her everything that she now knew. The woman was more a mother to her than what her own had been, and she treasured this book more than any other earthly possession that she owned. The very feel of the pages turning was a comfort to her when she knew that she needed help. She turned the pages now, searching for an age remedy. In the coldness of winter, Belle had started to feel aches in her joints, and her red hair was starting to lose its shine. She felt an anti-aging potion would perhaps help her chores go by faster in the morning. She flipped through the pages, scanning the recipes and stories. Then there it was: the recipe for the memory potion. She had been making it for Angelik. She had added a few things that she thought the angel would need. It would certainly be powerful. It had been meant to break down the barriers of magic that surrounded the child, as well as heal her real memory, so that she could tell them what had happened to her mother. It was never quite finished, and therefore could still be altered. She quickly flipped to a particularly potent recipe for awareness, which would awake someone from even the deepest of sleep.

She pondered it. Could this be the thing that Slatkin needed her to do? Could she awaken Evingh from his nightmares? She felt that she had to try.

Belle set to work, pulling out her herbs and spices. Even as the sun came up and her back ached with pain, she spread the ingredients out on the table. First was the aging potion. She had always despised the taste, but it would be worth it. It was actually a simple potion to make. For many, finding the proper ingredients was usually the hardest part. However, for her it was a task that she often performed, so they were readily available in her stores. She meticulously measured and weighed the small amount of matter that she had to work with until she held a small vial. Inside was a clear liquid that smelled sulfuric. She held her breath and swallowed. There was no immediate reaction, other than a need to vomit, but it soon passed.

Next was to make a new elixir for wakefulness that she could mix with the memory potion for Evingh. She examined the pages in the book. She needed the root of a baika vine, which she had a surplus of, and the seeds of a kial tree. Again, these were simple ingredients. The hardest part would be mixing the potions. In general, medicines were not to be crossed, but she knew that if it was done carefully and taken with the correct dosage, then it would be effective. She pulled the baika vine root and kial seed from the table and immediately started grinding the seeds in her mortar.

As she worked, she did not feel sleep creeping over her. Soon, she was sleeping at the table with the pestle and mortar still in her hands.

Then the dreams came. Part memory, part wish, all dream. She lay on the ground, in a bed of short grass, staring up at the millions of bright stars shining above her. She inhaled a breath of fragrant summer breeze and smiled. She looked over at Slatkin who lay with his hands crossed behind his head. Both of them were much younger. The wrinkles that she now carried had not yet begun to trace their way onto her face. Slatkin's hair still gleamed white, but his face was much younger. His eyes stared at the stars and reflected their shine.

"Your tales of the stars," she said, "I've not heard them anywhere else. I've looked through all the books in the library and haven't been able to find them anywhere."

"The true tales have been twisted to fit the fate that mankind has chosen for itself, but mine is true. I promise. I would never lie to you." He turned then to look at her. Her heart raced in her chest and she felt light headed.

"I believe you," she whispered. Her heart felt like it was in her throat and she could not speak any louder now. Slatkin smiled and turned away. She felt that he sensed her blushing at his gaze. She turned back to the stars, frustrated at having no control over her emotions. In the next moment, his face was over hers. His look was serious and intense.

"Belle," he said but before he could speak, she lifted her lips to his. There was no way to describe the feeling that followed, the rush of passion and wanting, of love and life, and freedom, and the unraveling of emotion that poured from within her. It lasted much longer than she had remembered. He ran his hands through her hair, something he often did whenever she let it down. It was her that pulled away this time. It had always been him before.

"What's wrong?" he asked. She knew then it was a dream. And she was quickly ripped back to reality. She breathed a heavy sigh upon awakening. Realizing that she had fallen asleep at the table, she ceased work for the evening and climbed the stairs to her chamber. She checked on Evingh and then headed to her own bed, where sleep took her quickly.

The dreams continued, but they turned dark. She was a young girl again, twelve years old. She was standing in the meadow picking wildflowers. She had come to be alone, but the other children had found her. She heard them walking behind her. She had planned to ignore them, but they walked behind her and without any words, they kicked her knees out from under her. She was wrestled to the ground, a black sack covered her face, and the beating for the day began. She never knew exactly how many taunted her, but there were many. They all pelted her will sticks and small branches.

Witch, witch

in the ditch

knock her down with a switch

witch witch

in the ditch

beat her down before she can snitch

Their taunts, which started slow, got faster and louder as the children beat her with their switches. Many of them chose ones with thorns especially for her. She had given up on fighting back. It would be a daily routine whether or not she fought them. She had come to accept it. She lay still so many days, at the edge of consciousness. Today was no different. When the children had used every insult that they could dream up to harm her, after their spitting and beating had ceased, they had left her alone. She came to long enough to pull the sack from over her face and stare up at the sky, only to see that she was late again for her schooling. No matter. She didn't want to go anyway. She passed out, and when she awoke, she stood and continued gathering the wildflowers and singing to herself. Though, it felt more like a task now, with her body feeling so bruised, and blood spilling from various tiny stabs and scratches left by the thorns. When her basket was full, she turned to limp back home, though she dreaded that as much as she dreaded school. Then her memory became dream and wish again. Slatkin was there, in the meadow of her homeland.

"Belle!" She heard his sorrow in the tone with which he said her name. "Belle, why do you let them do this to you every day?"

"Fighting back only makes it worse," she said. "They'll just beat me harder, or think of some new torture. At least the switches do not kill."

He held out his hand to her. She stumbled to him, and when he opened his palm, there was a flower, pink and in full bloom. "A gift of Sark," she said.

"A gift of healing," he said.

"Its power is less than a kiss," she said glancing hopefully at him.

Slatkin smiled. "I know, dear Belle, but it is more than my kiss. I wish to heal you, not bury you."

She took the flower in her palm, holding to his hand as she did so. She did not wish to wake now, but it was time. Her heart was heavy as she was torn from the dream world once again.

She checked the sky. It was already late into the night. She checked on Evingh. He was already awake. She only knew because he was sitting up in the bed, his eyes open, staring straight ahead.

"Up already, are you, dear?" She walked over to him and helped him from the bed. "Come with me, and we'll get your breakfast," she said. She assessed her feelings and smiled. The anti-aging potion had surely worked. The pains were less tonight than the last. She took Evingh's hand and led him to the kitchens. Tonight, she would finish the potion and she hoped that it would change him, that it would pull him from his dreams and transform him into the boy Evingh for good.

XIII: Interrogation

Galan heard only the sounds of many feet walking over the earth. His captors did not speak to him, they just pushed him forward. When his boot struck wood, he was thrust forward and shoved to the floor. A yell of pain erupted from his throat, as the arrow in his leg seemed to dig further into his flesh. He felt hands on him, taking the weapons from his sides. He felt them tying his arms to something, stretching his muscles. He was slowly lifted off of the floor. The pain from the arrow intensified. There was a long silence, and then a woman spoke. Her voice was deep and commanding.

"Are you a hunter?" she asked him. He wasn't sure how to answer her. He had been a hunter, but with the betrayal of Volkhan, he was unsure if he still could be proclaimed a hunter. He couldn't answer. He was struck then, sudden and violently across the side of his face. He thought to himself: *I have endured worse.* It was a hard hit, but it did not bother him the way that he was bothered when Volkhan struck him. He could taste blood welling in his mouth. The taste was metallic and unappealing. He spat it out.

A woman's hand grabbed his face. Her touch was rough and hard, not what he expected from someone with such small hands. When she spoke, he could tell that she was a younger woman, perhaps a child. Her voice was smooth and higher pitched. "When the Mother asks a question of you, you answer her immediately. She does not have time to be disrespected!" She shoved his face away from her.

Again, the woman with the deep voice, the one that he now assumed was the Mother, asked him the same question. "Are…You…A hunter?"

He felt himself trying to say yes, but wanting to say no. It came out as a grumble under his breath. Again, he was pummeled with a heavy blow. It was so strong that he was sure he blacked out for a moment.

As he tried to bring himself to, he felt his hands being untied and then he was grabbed and pulled down. He felt the wooden planks beneath him as he was drug across the floor and forced up and then downward…far into the ground. He heard the sound that his own body made as it thudded against wood. And there followed a quiet and a coolness. For a moment, his pain was so intense that he could not breathe. His head was spinning. When his breath came back to him, he desperately felt around him as best as he could with his hands still tied, and the blindfold still on. There was only wood. The space was small. It wasn't large enough for anyone else to fit into. He reasoned that it was some sort of a small prison cell. He thought then of his sister. He hoped that she was not suffering the same fate as him. He spit the blood from his mouth and then yelled to her, hoping that she would hear him.

"Kaila!" There was no response. "Kaila!" Again, he yelled, but there was only silence to answer him. He could feel the soreness in and around his mouth and on the side of his head when he yelled. The pain in his leg seemed to be moving through his muscles, making him feel weak. He assumed the arrow was poisoned. He needed to call out to her again. "Kaila. You are not a hunter! Tell them you are not a hunter! Kaila!" There was still no response, so Galan then began desperately trying to remove the blindfold from his head and the ropes from his hands, positioning himself against the wall of wood so that he could wiggle the blindfold off of his head. After struggling for a moment, he was able to loosen the blindfold away from his eyes. It fell to the floor beside him. Even with the blindfold gone, there was nothing to see. Everything was dark.

Kaila was being led away from the others. She could hear them fall away in the distance, but the dart was affecting the way she was seeing and feeling everything.

"Where are they going?" she heard herself asking. Her voice was slow and heavy sounding.

"They must go speak to the Mother, but you and I will come in here," her captor said. She felt herself walking on wood now instead of earth beneath her feet. Her blindfold came off, the rope was untied, and she was immediately offered a seat. The woman motioned to a cushion that sat on the floor by a pit of fire. Kaila took the seat, clumsily falling into it. The room was spinning with warmth, sweet aroma, and fire. The fire was calming. There was the sound of beautiful music in the distance.

"Are you a hunter?" the woman asked.

Kaila nodded. "I will be a powerful huntress one day. Just like my mother was."

"Well that is bold of you to look so far into the future!"

"It's true!" Kaila said. "My mother was training me. I can already skin the animals."

"A good skill in any village to be sure!" the woman replied. "Do you know that I had learned such things by your age as well. In a way, I am like you. I was taught to skin the animals, scale the fish, and prepare them for eating. I cook many things for my tribe. That is my place here. The Mother, who leads us, she says that not even she can cook as well as I can. It is not all that I do, though. All Astrids must learn to defend themselves...the other tribes, they take us. They take us, and we are never seen again. They took my mother, and my sister, and my mother's sister, all in the same raid. All of them...gone. That is why we put you in cages and bind your hands. We are afraid that you are here to take us."

"But we are not!" said Kaila. She knew then that she should be crying at the memory that she was about to release, but something about the music and the warmth made her feel that it was all right to say it now, and not be bothered by it. "I have been taken...by my own tribe. They killed my mother and Havink. I was saved, though. My brother told them not to kill me and then...a girl, like me, she saved me, and then the old man, he brought us here."

"Why did they take you?" she asked, puzzled by the news.

Kaila shook her head. "I don't know. I don't understand why they killed my mother and Havink. The strange man and his woman did it, but Volkhan, my father, he's the one that told them to. It's his fault and I'm going to kill him!" she exclaimed.

The woman was silent for a moment, but then she whispered. "What will you use?"

Kaila reached for her Valka blade, but realized that she did not have it. "I had a blade, a Valka blade." She felt her face redden and her eyes sting. "I was going to use the Valka blade that my mother carved for me!"

The woman nodded and then reached into a pouch at her side. She pulled the blade out. "I took it from you because I thought you were here to take us. Since you are so young, and it is special to you, then I will give it back."

Kaila took the valka blade with a smile.

The woman smiled back. "It is a fine blade that she made you. It is worthy of the task that you have made for yourself, if you still choose to do so when the time comes."

Khali hung her head in shame.

"Are you a hunter?" the voice asked her. Khali shook her head vigorously.

"No, never!" She could not contain her tears now. "I have never been a hunter...this is my home. You are my sister. Why do you treat me this way?"

"If you are a sister, then why do you stink of hunters?"

"Because I was taken by them!" Khali sobbed and thought of her son. If she did not save him soon, he would be killed. The Astrids would not let a hunter live. "I promise you. It is the truth! My son, he is here with us. He appears to be a hunter, but I promise you that he is not. He was born to a hunter, but I promise you that I have raised him to be like us. Please let me see him."

There was silence. Her blindfold was removed. "You have our stones on your bracelet. You still carry your sacred stones," the woman said to her. Khali could see that the stones of both Saigolai and Kialo glowed. "You are protected by the gods. You will not be killed. I cannot say the same for your son. That is up to the Mother." At her words, Khali's exhaustion set in, and she pleaded with every ounce of strength in her. "Please take me to him!"

The other woman nodded her head. "I will do that!"

Slatkin sat still. "You are not a hunter. You are not one of us. You are something else...perhaps sent by a god. Which god do you belong to?"

"I am a son of Saigolai."

"Why does Saigolai protect hunters? One would think Khanhine would do that himself!"

"Saigolai values all life and the ones that I protect are no longer hunters. They have been exiled for betraying their tribe. The woman is of your lineage, born as an Astrid. The boy is her son, born to her from a hunter. The girl was born of two hunters, but she is the half-sister of the

142

boy. Because he saved her life, he has betrayed his own kind. We come here seeking refuge and peace. We do not know where else to go. I cannot take them where the hunters can find them. They are sought now for a fate worse than death. I beg of you to hear our tale. You can then choose to let us pass through your land or to take us in, with the blessings of my father…if you choose to kill us, then you will all be cursed by Saigolai."

"Then we must go speak to the Mother. She is the one who has control of your fates." Quickly, the woman removed his blindfold and sliced through the ropes binding his hands. "Follow me," she said.

XIV: The Mother

The Astrid, who Slatkin learned was named Teehara, led him to an enormous round, wooden structure located in the center of the village. It was surrounded by walkways and a circular path, which led to several other paths leading in various directions. The hut was made of the kial wood, and woven strands from the more tender shoots had been stretched as a covering for a roof. They had to mount several steps to reach the door. Inside the hut, tapestries and valka furs insulated the walls, covering every space. In the center, the floor had been removed, and a fire pit made of large, black stones held red, flaming embers, creating a red glow around them. A strong, perfumed smoke wafted through the room from the fire. At the farthest side of the hut, a great staircase led up to a dais, where the Mother sat. She was flanked on either side of her throne by two guards.

Slatkin approached the Mother with respect. She was the reining ruler of the Astrids. In general, they were a peaceful tribe, though he had assumed that they would have been greeted with less hostility upon entering the borders. *Another way the world is changing...* he thought. After the Astrid who led him here had spoken, the mother motioned for Slatkin to be brought to her. She smiled at him with a hard and wizened face. One of her teeth glowed white from between her wrinkled lips. Her skin was dark, and her hair was white. Surprisingly, it lay smooth and natural, unlike the other women they had encountered with masks. She was dressed in clothes that had been adorned with many of the rocks that Khali had worn on her bracelet, though there were more stones decorating the Mother than could be counted. Some were pierced to her flesh, some were on numerous bracelets and necklaces. They were even made into adornments on her leather clothes. The largest ones were fashioned onto her belt, a crown of kial wood that she wore on her head, and a staff which she held in her right hand. All of Saigolai's stones burned bright white and emitted a humming sound as Slatkin neared the bottom of the stairs.

"A son of Saigolai," she said, her voice was deep and rough. "What is it that he commands of us?"

"I have come to return one who was taken from you, and ask that you either accept her and the two children with open arms, or allow us all to pass unharmed."

The mother sat back as if in deep contemplation. Several colors of stones lit up, some brighter than others. A troubled look crossed the old woman's face. She shook her head as she spoke, deeply troubled. "The boy is being pursued. He has a much-coveted gift."

Slatkin nodded his head. "He saved the young girl. I knew then, when he fooled Nometheog, that he would be hunted by the gods. Saigolai has sent me to protect both children. Saigolai wishes only for life to be long and prosperous. He does not wish harm upon anyone. He will protect you if you will allow them to stay."

The Mother nodded her head. "Yes, this I will do…for now, but the hunters *will* find him. Nometheog has them tamed to his ways. Even Khanhine cannot control them now. The hunter god has lost many of his children to Nometheog…as all things are lost to darkness…and the boy can only stay for a short time. He must leave. It is our way. He does not belong here. He belongs with the men, way over on the shoreline. The Wards will help him to tame his gift. We women do not fully understand the gifts when they go to the men. The rocks on the shoreline will speak to him, like the ones in the mountain speak to me. But the woman, Khali, she belongs here, and though her gift has been stolen, we will find a use for her. Perhaps she can serve me here in the Mundara-Hut." The Mother paused then, nodding her head as if having a conversation in her mind. Then she looked at the dark angel and continued. "The little girl...she is young. She can be taught our ways. Even if she is a hunter, she is young enough still to be shown another way. I will take her as a daughter. She will be a Hungawki, my personal daughter. The other women will not like it, but I will see that she is protected and respected among the tribe."

"I thank you, as does Saigolai," Slatkin said. The Mother nodded and spoke to one of the women that stood guard by her throne. She spoke in the native Astrid tongue. The masked woman, who carried a wooden staff, walked up the stairs to where the Mother sat and then behind her chair. She pulled open a large, wooden door that opened into the floor. The Mother looked seriously at Slatkin.

"My apologies to the boy," she said, "but we thought he was a hunter. I was rash and brutal. I may need your assistance in pulling him free."

Puzzled, Slatkin walked up the stairs and stared below into the dark pit where Galan had been thrown.

He glared a moment at the Mother then turned to the boy. "Are you alright?" he asked. It was more of a consolation to the boy, rather than a question. Slatkin knew that he was not alright.

"Kaila!" Galan called with slowed speech, an effect of the poison. His voice came from far beneath. "…and my mother. Where are they?" he asked, his voice dry and weak. His eyes squinted at the light that filtered down to him.

"They are faring much better than you!" Slatkin exclaimed. "I'm coming to get you!" Slatkin then requested rope. The Astrid guard provided it for him. After taking off the silver fur coat to reveal a black tunic, he tied the rope around his waist and asked the woman to lower him into the pit. It was far enough down that Slatkin was glad he was being lowered instead of falling. He edged his way down to the bottom, dim light shown from high above. He felt for holds within the wood as he was lowered, but the wood remained smooth all the way to the bottom. Slatkin looked down at Galan, who had tried to make room for the angel in the tiny pit.

When he saw the bruises and swollen eye on Galan's face, he was pained to look at it. "I'm sorry that I was not here. I thought that they would be kinder to you, but a lot is changing in the world. I promised that nothing would happen to you, but it did. Can you forgive me, Galan?" Slatkin was sincere. He never promised anything unless he could follow through with it, but there was a first for everything...

Galan just nodded his head.

"From my reasoning," Slatkin started, "we were all in different places, but your mother and Kaila are being escorted here to see us now." It was such a tight fit in the space that it was hard to maneuver with two people, but Slatkin managed to help Galan to stand up. He was having trouble with the leg that had been shot with the arrow. When he finally stood beside Slatkin, the orostiro was able to help him hold to the rope above him, and then they yelled for the guard to pull them out. Slatkin held to the bottom of the rope, using his feet to climb, securing any fall that Galan would have. Once out into the Mother's hut, Galan lay on the floor, out of breath and wincing in pain. Slatkin looked to the Mother. "We must heal him," he said.

She nodded her head. "That we must. You all need healing." She looked at him, straight into his eyes as if she knew what he was thinking. It unnerved him and he wondered if this is how the humans felt when he looked into their soul. "Do not tell me, son of Saigolai, that you are not in need of healing as well. You would be denying the truth. We will heal you all. This I promise!" She then turned to the other guard and spoke to her in Astrid language.

The Mother looked at them and smiled, one of the stones glowed in her smile, replacing a tooth. "Tonight, you will heal and then I have questions for Khali and both of the children. After that, you will hear my tales." She laughed a cackling aged laugh, laughing at some joke that only she seemed to understand. "Get them to Talomna, the healer!" she exclaimed to her guards. They were quick to lift Galan to his feet. Slatkin offered to help him. He seemed to be almost unconscious, leaning against the angel.

He was cold and pale. Sweat had broken out on his forehead. Slatkin urged him forward and they left the hut with the guards. The sound of the Mother's cackling could be heard as they were escorted out.

XV. Nightmares

Evingh drank the mixture. She knew he would. It would take a few hours to fully take effect. In the meantime, she read to him by the fire in her quarters. For a long time, he was expressionless as usual, but gradually, she noticed that his brows started to furrow and his mouth turned into a frown. Eventually as she read, he began mumbling. She put the book down and looked at him.

"Evingh?" she asked.

An earsplitting scream was his reply.

He was weeping, almost convulsing in his distress. She reached out to him to take him into her arms to console him.

"Oh, Evingh, I'm sorry. Whatever it is, it's better now. It's all better. I'm here." She said things like this over and over but he continued to wail and scream. He never spoke, but he was making a sound of torment, shaking all over, curled next to her with wide eyes, then when he closed them, he wept until there were no more tears. She just held to him, wondering if his pain was something of her doing or if it was something that Slatkin had done to him. Celeste claimed that he was living in a nightmare of his own making.

Belle became upset then. He had been sedated for a reason. She had done nothing to help him. She had only made things more difficult on herself. She should have known better than to try to undo Slatkin's work. She stared down at him, reminded of children throwing fits for no reason, though, there was always a reason. Again, she reached out to him, to console him. He pushed her away and writhed away from her, his face turning red from the fearful scream escaping him. Belle felt tears welling in her own eyes.

"Evingh," she said, in her motherly tone, "Please, Evingh, you are good, and I know it. I'm not going to hurt you, it's Belle. I'm here to help you, Evingh..." she watched him, curled in a corner with his arms covering his face. "Please, listen to me, I promise I will help you. I promise!" She approached him carefully this time, slowly.

"Evingh, it's Belle. I'm here. I here, Evingh, to help you," She spoke calmly. Her voice was low and caring. "Please let me help you, Evingh. He gave a small jerk at the touch of her hand, but then he was still, as she reached out again to him. The tears had stopped and he just stared ahead again.

For a moment, she thought that he had lapsed back into a catatonic state, but then he looked at her and for once, she saw some emotion in his eyes. The look that he gave her cut right through her soul. It was truly a tortured expression.

"Evingh, I'm here and I won't hurt you. Whatever it is that you're thinking or remembering, it is all gone now."

He looked away again, down at the floor. She reached down to embrace him and he fell into her arms, silently weeping. She felt his tears leaking through her dress. She dared not move or speak, for fear that the fit would return.

She patted and rubbed his back and shoulders, and ran her fingers through his light brown hair. He lay in her arms, like a child weeping in his mother's embrace.

She dared not stir for a long time. She let him weep until he exhausted himself, and eventually, he fell back into a real sleep. When she felt she would not disturb him, she left to gather a blanket and a pillow for him. She left him where he lay, but placed the pillow under his head and made sure that his body was covered with the blanket. He rested, though it was uneasy. He mumbled and called out several times. She stayed close, only leaving when necessary. She kept the fire roaring in the fireplace to keep him warm, and she had gathered the pot of stew from the kitchen and brought it to her fire to warm it up. She knew that he'd be hungry upon awakening.

She sat there, trying to watch over him, trying to watch for any sign of new change in him. She had hardly began dreaming when she woke. Evingh was crying again, though he seemed to still be asleep. She could tell by the expression on his face that he was in some emotional turmoil. The blanket she had given him was soaked with sweat. She brushed his hair from his face.

"Shhh, it's okay now, Evingh. I'm here." Still sleeping, he grabbed her hand with both of his and pulled it to his cheek. A few moments later, he awoke with a start, pushing her away.

He stared around at his surroundings and grabbed his head as if it hurt, then he covered his eyes with hands. Belle spoke softly again. "I'm here, Evingh," she said.

She jumped with surprise when he spoke, "I..." his voice was course and cracked after not using it for so many days. "I told them not to run."

"What?" she asked. "Who, Evingh, who did you tell not to run?"

He looked at her but she knew that he was still dreaming. The blank look had come back to his eyes. "They were running with candles, and now I don't even know where they are. I need to make it back to them. They've nothing to eat!"

He said the words and then fell back onto the pillow. Raspy coughing breaths escaped from him and his chest rose heavily up and down then he was sleeping soundly again.

Belle breathed heavily. She didn't know how much more of this she could take. She left the room to get her cookbook. She wanted a cure for nightmares. She knew that she should wait for Slatkin, but she could not handle Evingh if he acted this way. She couldn't bear to watch this suffering.

Later

Belle sat at the kitchen table. Evingh was still sleeping, though she had wrestled him to the kitchen table. His head now lay on his arm, a bowl of stew, uneaten not far away. She sat now grinding sea shells into a fine powder. This potion would work, she knew that it would. It had to!

XVI. Healing

The healer was an older woman. It was hard to distinguish what exactly her face looked like. She had painted herself in paints that made her look different depending on how the light struck her face. From one angle, her skin would appear pale and young, from another angle, she appeared fierce and aged. She reached for Galan first and took him over to the remnants of a kial thieren stump that was as large as a bed. It had been hollowed out and filled with many small pebbles. Two other women assisted her here. They now draped a large animal hide over the stump. The healer gave the boy something to drink from a clay bowl. It made him sputter and cough. Then she helped him to lie on the stump. He lay there, breathing heavily. The assistants brought her various large stones which she placed strategically over the ailing parts of his body. She chanted and carefully ran her hands over injured places. At times, the stones would glow. If they did not, she cast them aside and yelled for another. As she chanted, the pebble bed lit up a warm glowing orange. The temperature in the hut increased until the others were shedding their own furs, sweat pouring down their foreheads. At times, she would call for herbs, oils, or animal bones. It seemed to go on for a long time. Finally, one of the assistants came to the others.

"There is much more to do for your friend, but she must take a break and let him dream. She is tired, so we will heal you three later. Come in here. We will give you food and rest while you wait." They stood and followed her to another room of the hut. There, more assistants brought food and the travelers were given places to rest. After eating, both Kaila and Khali were taken by healers. Eventually, the room cleared out, and only Slatkin remained. Even the healers had left.

He stepped out of the hut for a moment. The chill in the air was nice after being in the heated hut. His thoughts wandered for a moment. He anticipated the plans of the enemies. Where were they now? Had they crossed the river yet? How could he keep this boy safe? The Mother had warned him that she could not conceal them forever. He knew it to be true. They would have to leave soon...he was ready to leave. He cared for the welfare of these people, but his heart was not in his task the way that it should be. The Astrids had hurt the boy. He could have stopped it, but he admitted to himself that even then, on the bridge, his mind had been wandering…wandering too far. He had been thinking of her, his Belle. He pulled the pink flower out of his pocket. It's true, he should offer it to the healers, but he didn't want to. It was a selfish thing to keep this, but it made him think of her and even though it now lay withered in his hands, it was still something to remind him of Belle. A voice brought him away from his thoughts. The mother was standing near the hut, her many stones glowed in various colors, her wizened skin shining in the glow. She was leaning on her staff for support and she was smoking a large kial stick that burned brightly at the end, placed between her lips. She blew a large huff of smoke and then put her free hand out to him.

"Come, son of Saigolai," she said, her lips still hanging to the stick as she spoke. "I will heal you. You are beyond Talomna's skills." Slatkin stepped forward.

"What makes you think that you are up to the task?" he asked.

His words made the Mother chuckle. "I, like you, have been appointed by the gods. I must do what they tell me to. I am a servant, as are you."

Slatkin nodded his head. "Well then, I hope that my father is in a forgiving mood."

He followed the Mother back into the Mundara-hut. They walked into a different room than before, to the right of the dais where her throne stood. A similar stump to the one in the healer's hut was found in this new room, with the same small round pebbles. These were already alight with the orange glow.

The Mother insisted that Slatkin remove his shirt so that she could see the wounds on his chest and back.

After examining them, she puffed on her kial stick and holding it between two fingers, flipped the ashes onto the floor. "These are not too old to heal, as I had feared they would be. There is still hope for you," she said, peering then at his eyes. She placed her hand, still holding the kial stick on the wound in his chest. Galan's blade had pierced him there. "This will be the hardest. It is more than a blade that has wounded you here," she said, her voice deep. She smiled knowingly, the stones glowing where there should be teeth. "Saigolai has already been very forgiving with you. He insists that I use the flower. I need it for my ritual."

Slatkin's eyes narrowed. "Do you really?"

She nodded her head. "I cannot lie to you, and I cannot lie to the gods. You are all in my head at once anyway. If I lie, you will know it." She pointed to the bed of hot orange pebbles. "Rest now, and let me do my ritual."

He reluctantly followed her instruction, and reached into his pocket. He pulled the withering flower out, and handed it over to her with much reluctance. Then he lay down. Immediately, the heat from the rocks filled the pain in his back with a numbing relief. A sweet aroma followed; it was the scent of the flower. There was music now, low and melodic. It was calming. He was only now faintly aware that the Mother was tending the wound on his chest. The aroma, music, and heat were overpowering, and soon, he was unsure whether or not he was sleeping or having some vision from his father. His father was there, before him, holding the flower.

"We've been over your tasks, son. Many times, we've been over your tasks…" his words faded away into the music that was playing. He thought perhaps he heard a discussion between the hunters that were now stalking them.

"The river is never unfrozen at this time," the first one said.

"Some force moves the current against us," the other said.

Their voices faded to the rushing of the river currents, it drowned out the voices of everything, and there was the music again, and he was looking in on Belle. She was crying, looking between bottles in a box. "If only it was ready, this might help."

Then there was the Mother's voice. "It's okay to speak to her, you are not really there. Your father can do nothing now. It is only a dream."

Slatkin spoke then to Belle. "What are you looking for?"

Belle stopped sobbing then, and Slatkin reached out to wipe her tears. He found that the ability to read her soul was gone. He felt the tears, salty wet and as real as if he were awake and in the room with her. "Let me help you, Belle."

She exhaled then. "I just want the nightmares to stop," she said.

"Me too," he replied. Her hand landed on a bottle.

"I wonder if this would help…or would it make it worse?"

"Only you know, Belle," he said. "You made it."

She held it to her chest. "Yes," she nodded her head. "Yes, I think it will help."

Again, there was the rushing sound of the river, and Slatkin was with his father again. "Son, I do not ask too much of you. I have never given you a task that is beyond your abilities. If I thought you were not to be trusted, then I would handle the situation myself. I have always been able to trust you. It is your lack of concentration and dedication that keep you from succeeding. It has always been so."

Again, the Mother spoke. "You have to relax your mind, stop worrying about the mortals for now, you have time to really dream for once. Don't waste it." There was a tug on his chest. It wasn't pain, just a light pressure.

Then the rushing water again. Then he was back there with Belle. Only now, she was cleaning the kitchen. He went to help her as usual. They talked but he couldn't remember what had been spoken, for the scene soon turned. He pulled the black kerchief from her head, revealing the long layers of striking red hair. He could feel heat pulsing through his veins when he touched her. Her hair was like fire dancing in his hands. Her lips soon found his and the fire spread throughout his body as her hands moved over him. She left her hand resting on his chest and he felt her glow there. Her warm, healing glow was filling him. He saw her then, not losing her life, but gaining more as she healed him. She appeared younger and healthier the longer she held on to him. "This cannot be wrong. I'll never believe that it is," she said.

"This should kill you," he reasoned.

Her hand went over his lips. "See the truth. I would die without you."

Suddenly, and regretfully, he awoke. The Mother stood over him, her hand on his chest. "Your healing is difficult but possible. Rest now, and do not worry. The gods tell me that your Belle is safe." Slatkin could feel himself trembling, tears filled his eyes. The Mother covered him with a fur. "The heat is healing. You will feel better when you awaken." Slatkin started to protest, but she whispered a small chant and Slatkin was unable to stay awake any longer. He soon fell into a deep, restful sleep. It was free from dreams. The Mother kept watch over him, the gods silenced now, except Saigolai, who only wished his son to recover.

Galan awakened slowly. He felt rested, but stiffness remained in his muscles. When they tried to get him to sit up, it exhausted him, so they let him lay back down. Khali reached for his hand and lifted it to her lips to kiss him.

"I have been worried," she said.

He did not respond.

There was a calm quiet then as only the sound of the healer's music was heard.

"Where's Kaila?" he whispered.

"She will be here shortly," his mother said. Then, after contemplating his question, she asked her own.

"I understand your struggle to keep her safe," she started, "but what will you do when the time comes to leave her behind?"

"Who says that I'm leaving?" he asked.

"You cannot stay here, my son. It is dangerous. The hunters will find you here. You will travel across the land to the Wards. There you will gain power over your destiny."

Galan sighed heavily. He understood, but he didn't like it.

"But I promised Kaila that I would teach her what I know. I want her to fulfill her wish…I want her to kill him."

Khali nodded her head. "Perhaps the gods will do it for her."

He stared at his mother, his doubt showing in his expression.

She read the look knowingly. "She may yet get the chance, but she will learn her skills here. She will become worthy of the blade that she carries and when the time comes, she will be able to destroy him." She could tell that he was not convinced. "Besides, she will understand if you leave. The Astrids have already been over the plan with her. She is curious about the power you will gain. That is what you should look forward to…your power. A life with the Wards will give you the advantage over our enemies, including your father."

His mother had cajoled him back into a comfortable rest, and later in the day, Galan awoke to healers trying to get him to sit up. Galan did so with very stiff muscles. It was the kind of stiff that would go away with physical exertion. They helped him walk around the room until the stiffness passed and then he sat on a chair away from the bed of stones. His leg was still sore, but the healing stones had worked wonders on the wound.

"I want to thank you for healing me," he said to Talomna, who now looked young. "I don't think I could have made it to the Wards without you."

She smiled at him. "I thought that you would be a challenge, but it seems that the gods favor you. You are one of a kind."

"Why me?" he asked. "What makes me different?"

"It is your power," she said. "The gods, they wish to control you. Your gift is coveted among them."

"I keep hearing all these stories about my power, but I don't have any that I know of."

She nodded her head. "We all have power, everyone. Even you! You will see what it is soon enough. I do not know what it is and even if I did, I could not be the one to tell you. You will find out when the time is right. Then, and only then, will you understand."

Galan was left then in silence for several minutes. When Talomna came back, Kaila was with her. Kaila walked cautiously to her brother. He smiled when he saw her looking so healthy. The Astrids had freed her hair from its braids and it hung loose down her back. Galan reached out and wove the strands between his fingers.

"What's this?" he asked.

Kaila smiled. "They are getting me ready for a ceremony," she said. Her voice was louder and more confident than it had been in all the days since her mother's passing.

He looked then at Talomna as he spoke, daring her to intervene in his questioning. "What have they told you, Kaila…about me?"

"You're leaving. You're crossing the island to gain power."

He nodded his head. "You know this means that I can't keep my promise to you. Not for now anyway."

She nodded. "I know," she said. "You can teach me when you come back. Every spring, the Wards make a crossing of the lands and the river. They come here for the Lauming. You will not be old enough and neither will I, but you still get to make the crossing. You will see me in the summer."

"I'm okay with it if you want to stay here." He looked Kaila in the eyes. "But I can't leave you unless I know that YOU choose to stay here. Not this tribe, not the old man, but YOU!"

"I do, Galan. I choose this. These women…they are not my mother, but they…" he could tell that she was about to cry. Her words caught on her throat and tears welled in her glands. "They care for me the way that my mother did. They are good, I know it!"

It was hard for the boy to breathe now. He sighed heavily and nodded his head. He could think of no words to say to her at the moment. She reached out and took his hand. "Summer is not that far away. Maybe I'll have more practice by then anyway."

Galan just nodded his head. "I just want you to be safe!"

She smiled then. "I know. Don't worry. I'm safe here…and I might find my own power, the kind like these women have…and like my mother had."

"I hope you do," he said, sincerity traced into every contour of his expression. She withdrew her hand and turned to the Astrid who stood beside her. They left the room as quietly as they had entered. Galan scowled. He thought about everything that had happened over the last few days. His life was so different from what it used to be. So little time had passed, and yet it seemed ages ago when he had first left his home with the other hunters. He felt that he was not himself…or was it that he truly felt himself? Now that he was free from the fear that his father would hurt his mother or himself. He knew though, that he would have to leave his mother soon…and his sister. The thought was heavy in his head. The healers soon came back to have him walk more. He cast aside his emotions as he focused on walking alone. The pain nagged in his leg, but it was nothing. He had overcome worse. If they were going to leave, he felt it should be sooner rather than later. After all, he wanted to be done with the whole thing. If he was to cross the island, he'd rather do it now than later.

XVII. The Scithronians

The night passed quickly for the angels as they reminisced with Saltook about the ways of the old kingdom. All too soon, though, they realized that they must be moving on. Without any words to the sleeping Scithronians upstairs, they said their goodbyes, content with Saltook's pledge of loyalty and aid.

The normal routine for dark angels would be to rest in the day, but they dared not rest, knowing how short their time was. They traveled quickly, with the pale sunlight glowing in a white circle beyond the clouds of a winter sky. They traveled as quickly as the horses could carry them. Victor often slowed in pace behind the others. In these times, Celeste would slow her horse to fall in beside him. She knew in these times he was experiencing her past. However unfair it seemed to them both, she understood the necessity. He would gain power to bring justice to the hunters. She often reached out, with her hand over his as they held the reins. When they stopped for a break, she tied his reins to her horse.

After nightfall, they approached the Scithronians. Alexandria dismounted, and the angels stopped. There was faint rustling in the branches. Alexandria remembered her first encounter with this tribe. They had been meaning to rob her, but instead they had treated her to a feast, realizing who she was. Her coming had been foretold by their seer Klarrissa. She wondered if the seer had foreseen their coming again. As if reading her thoughts, the seer appeared before them, stepping out from the roots of a kial tree. Her bright red bangs could be seen beneath the fabric of her hood. Her eyes stared at them, blue for the moment. She was young, as were all the Scithronians.

Celeste recognized her right away and dismounted to run to her. Wrapping her arms around the young woman's neck with joy, she exclaimed, "Klarrissa? I'm so glad to see that you survived!"

When she released the seer, the young woman fell to the ground in a low bow. "My queen!" she exclaimed. Tears fell from her eyes as she spoke. "I hoped that my visions were true. I hoped for so long that it was not a lie of the darkness!"

Celeste kneeled down to her. "Please stand and speak with me," she said.

Klarrissa stood, taking in the sight of her queen. "I saw that you would come back to us, but I did not see the means. I did not know where you were. You were lost!"

Celeste nodded her head. "Yes, Sark was lost to me. I could not feel any of you from the land of my imprisonment, either." She smiled with joy as she looked at Klarrissa. "I must greet all of you," she said. "There is much that we must accomplish!"

The seer took her hands. "Come with me and I will show you the meager means of our survival."

Celeste motioned for the others to follow her. Barrett, the keeper of the horses, was quick to see to their animals. Smiling as Alexandria's unicorn gladly went with him. He had taken extra good care of the animal the last time it was in his care. He had earned the trust of the animal and it made him proud.

Once the horses had been seen to, the angels followed the seer into the den of the Scithronians. They walked into the hollowed trunk of a kial thieren and stepped down the rungs of a ladder into a warm and inviting atmosphere beneath the surface of the land. Two long tables were aligned along the wall with chairs and benches pulled up along the sides. Torches burned warm and bright in sconces attached by iron brackets into the black roots of the tree, which made up the walls of the tunnels. Klarrissa motioned to the table.

"It's by no means the throne that I would wish to offer, but please have a seat. I have my cooks preparing something for you. The elves are here as well. They bring news for you, though they would not tell me what. We had to ask them to help us with this feast. Our stores are low and there would not have been enough to last us through the winter. The elves often help us."

Celeste laughed. "They helped me as well. I would not be here today without the help of their prince. I owe him more than I can ever repay him."

"He helped you escape?" The seer asked.

"Yes," she said. "And I will always be grateful for that."

"Then you must be prepared to help us find him." The voice came from a doorway across the room. All the heads in the room turned to see an elf entering the threshold. Though she wore traveling clothes, she radiated an ethereal light about her, and her black hair seemed to shimmer with stars from a night sky. The angels recognized her as Arista, princess of the moon elves.

"It is because he helped you that we have lost him," Arista said. "I too have been banished in a way. I left the land of Shea forever. I can no longer go back to live under the tyranny of Kristiniva. I would rather banish myself, and commit my time to finding my brother, than to live an eternity forgetting him, never even able to utter his name."

Celeste was visibly upset at her words. She shook her head.

Victor hurried, walking to hold Celeste's trembling hands. "I should have killed her when I had the chance," he said, turning to Arista. "We will help you find him. I promise."

XVIII. Tales of the Mother

Later in the day, Galan was resting again, when the Mother came to see him. She hurried the healers out of the room and came to stand by him. He didn't know if he should be afraid of her, or if he should trust her. She hurried the last healer out and then turned to face him. Her aged smile slid across her face with new wrinkles forming over her cheeks.

"You, my son, are no longer a hunter, but you have been. Tell me, what lore do you know of the god Khanhine?"

"I've heard many things," he said, "sometimes different versions of the same tale." The Mother nodded her head.

"Yes, yes. It is my guess that your mother and father told them to you?"

He nodded.

"And the tales varied depending on who told them, am I right?"

He nodded once more.

"Tell me now what you have heard…about the Khanhine-lupa. What does your father tell you? What are they? How are they made?"

"My father says that many years ago, before he was born, the hunters ran along-side Khanhine. He showed them how to hunt the animals, and how to prepare them. He even taught them how to cook them. They would hunt with him, and feast in his hall, but not all of them. He chose the best from among them to learn his ways, and entrusted them to share the power with the others. They were the chosen tribal leaders. A time came when Khanhine called on his hunters to follow him. One of them refused. Newly paired with his lover, he wished only to stay with her. To convince him to go, Khanhine placed a curse on the woman. He turned her into a wolf. She immediately bounded away, into the forest, and away from her lover. He chased after her as Khanhine laughed. "Once a hunter, you are bound to me, and a hunter you will always be," Khanhine yelled after the hunter, who now followed the tracks of his wife. Along the way, however, he met the god Saigolai, giver of life. Saigolai promised that if the hunter would follow him that he would spare his wife, and although he could not undo what Khanhine had done to her, he could turn him into a wolf also. So, the two lovers lived as wolves, missing their old life, but glad to be together. The female soon gave birth. Her child was both wolf and woman. They raised her as well as they could. When the woman grew, she discovered her origins, and spent her life luring the children of Khanhine to their deaths. It was vengeance against Khanhine for the cruel trick he had played on her parents. It is said that through the generations, she has lured many hunters away from their path, either by luring them to their deaths, or into mating with her, by which she has spawned creatures like her throughout the land. Her cruelest trick is that if they ever kill her children, they also kill theirs. Khanhine-Lupah are dangerous creatures, appearing to be wolves sometimes, and humans at others. There are rewards for killing them. It is said that if the mother of the beasts can be killed, then the rest will perish."

The Mother's face was hard to read as he told the tale. "And how does one kill the Khanhine-lupah?" she asked.

"There are two ways," he said. "One is to kill a child of Saigolai and take their power. That will destroy anything. The other is…" He was afraid to tell the Mother the other, but he decided that it was better to tell her than to keep a secret from her. She would be formidable. "Well, it is said that if a hunter mates with an Astrid, they can take her gift and be able to recognize the Khanhine-lupah from regular wolves and people. That will allow them to have the advantage and kill the beasts."

The Mother nodded her head. "The hunters understand many things, but that is not how we learn the story. It is true that a hunter can take the gift of an Astrid…but not all Astrids have the gifts that the hunters desire."

"My father says that they still make the best wives. They have magic."

The Mother grinned. Many stones glowed in her mouth, in the place of where her teeth should be. "We are magical, but not the way they think."

"I know," said Galan, "My mother has told me. There is no real magic, just knowledge and spirit-gifts, though she says that Volkhan stole her gift from her."

The Mother's grin faded. "That part is true. Your mother, she is a powerful woman in heart. Quick-witted and strong, but her spirit gift has left her. I see it in her eyes...or rather, I don't. There is nothing there to see anymore."

"And what was her gift?" Galan asked.

The Mother shook her head. "She never told you?"

Galan shook his head. "She rarely speaks of it and when I ask her, she quickly finds things to keep her busy or avoids the subject."

"It is a terrible thing to have your gift stolen. Especially when it could help so many...but these things are not for me to discuss with you. Your mother has her reasons for silence."

Later in the evening, an event was being held outside. A large fire had been built in the center of the Astrid village. The tribe had all gathered by it, wrapped in furs, they sat anxiously awaiting the Mother. Galan had been allowed to join. The healers had brought him out and helped him find a comfortable spot. He sat, leaning against a small tree. The youngest of the healers, Wishkasa, was tending to him now. She had never spoken to him. She never chanted any of the tunes that the others did as she healed him, though she stared at him the most intensely. The feeling he got sometimes as she stood over him made him uneasy, but when she closed her eyes, or if he looked away, he could rest. He thought at first that she was shy, but the other healers assured him that she had never spoken. As they sat waiting for the Mother, she opened a small bottle of paint. It had a deep black pigment. She dipped her pinkie into the paint, and rubbed it along her face. She drew circles and strange shapes. Galan was going to ask her what she was doing, but he knew that she would not respond. When she looked at him and held out the bottle, he shook his head. She smiled, dipped her pinkie in, and reached out to his face. He jerked away from her hand, and her smile widened. She persisted and at her touch, he sat still. She drew designs on his face. He felt ridiculous, but everyone else seemed to have used paint on their faces as well. He felt himself unable to turn away from her at the moment. Her eyes did not stare directly into him, but instead he could tell that she was thinking about what she was painting. He decided that he liked looking at her eyes when she was not staring into his.

"Your eyes have a curious look," he said "I'm terrified at their beauty," it was out before he could bite his tongue. He immediately wished that he could take it back but he had already said it, in Astrid, so there was no mistaking it for her.

She stopped painting and just looked at him. Her look of concentration faded, and there was something else there. It was emotion that he could not place. He immediately found himself apologizing in Astrid. "I'm sorry. I should not have said that."

She smiled again then covered his lips with her hand and shook her head. Galan took a deep breath. He wished that she could speak. He didn't know now whether she was telling him not to apologize or not to speak at all. He decided the latter would keep him out of the most trouble. When she was done painting, she sat back with a satisfied look on her face, then she left him. He wondered which one of the healers would come to take her place.

When the Mother came out, it was quite a show. She wore a large bird mask with black feathers leading down her back. The eyes on the mask seemed to glow in the firelight and the bird seemed to be peering down at them all, judging them from within. Some of the Astrids began to play music, and the Mother placed herself on a dais before the large fire so that they could all see her. Then the music ended and her deep voice cackled, somehow amplified from within the bird mask.

"Hear, hear, the tale of our beginnings.

A tale of gods, a tale of men.

There was once only one god

but he divided himself

and became the first four

The greater gods are and always have been

They are Saigolai, Sari, Nometheog, and Vishka

Saigolai the god of life paired himself

with Sari, goddess of healing,

together they made all Earths.

to counter them were Nometheog, god of the void

and Vishka, the goddess of suffering.

There were many battles in the beginning

for each time Saigolai created

Nometheog would un-create

Then Sari would heal the wounds

And Vishka would make them wish it to end.

That was their way.

Then Saigolai devised a plan. He created an earth

and there Sari would stay, becoming formless and

all-powerful, it was a land of healing.

And there, the creatures of Saigolai would thrive.

All manner of creatures were created there,

some of which are lost to our lore.

The tales of that land are all but lost

except for the knowledge of the lesser gods.

It was there that Saigolai paired with his lover

to create the lesser gods. They had many children

The first was Selfirin, a god of light

It was he who pushed Nometheog

from most worlds

by filling every void with his light

so that Nometheog could not undo it.

The second was Kialo, a god of earth that helped

to bring about all the flowers and the trees.

Kristiniva was the weather goddess and she

would ensure that the fields and flowers

of her lover would never die. They soon paired.

Then there were Adrianna

daughter of Kialo and Kristiniva

and Dracinus, son of Saigolai

The Mother of the Ocean and Father of Ice

Together they sustain the worlds

with healing and preservation

Then there was Thiera, and Khanhine

Thiera filled the mountains with fire

And showed the humans how to use her gift to

bring light when natural darkness came.

Khanhine was next, showing the humans how

to hunt the animals of Kialo.

For Kialo created them

to sustain the children of the Earth.

Saigolai had many children after,

for as a god of life

he must always create. His children help us

in our everyday struggle, as we all strive

to live in light, free of Nometheog's darkness."

The Mother then removed her mask, which as she spoke had lit up with reflections of the fire. The mask that had at first been black became various colors as she had thrown dusts on the fire, making it spark in reds, greens, blues, and purples. Now she stood as a woman. "There are many tales of the gods, and we all know that Kialo shaped us from the clay and Saigolai gave us our breath so that we could live on the earth. The tales stretch throughout a vast time, but the tale that I have for you tonight is one of truth. It is one of Khanhine and the Khanhine-lupah."

Khanhine used to live among us.

He was the first hunter, a child of Saigolai

created to teach the children of Earth

how to sustain their lives.

Hunting was a sacred ceremony

He warned that if not done properly,

it would invite the children of Nometheog

and Vishka

into the world that we belong to.

For all life is sacred, even that of the beasts.

The Khanhine-Lupa were created
when Khanhine took a human wife,
for his former lover, Hawitha
a goddess of gathering crops
had been locked away
by dark forces of the opposing side.
The mother was tended to by many
including newer children of Saigolai.
But when she gave birth
the thing born to her was not like a human,
nor was it like a god.
It was part beast and part human.
When the hunters saw it, they tried to kill it.
They killed its Mother and the animal itself
was helped by the children of Saigolai,
for it would always be hunted by its own kind.
Both humans and beasts.
Khanhine was so upset by the slaying of his lover
that he turned on his followers.
He protected his child and trained it well.
It grew to a woman and she found a human lover
And had children. The Khanhine-lupah.

Now the hunters can only become true

If they hunt with these children

but to do so they must tell the difference

between the children and the beasts.

A feat they have yet to master.

Without the knowledge of Khanhine

they are left in darkness and denial.

Unable to fulfill their purpose

they are godless and abandoned.

left to the forces of darkness.

for to be without a god,

one accepts the void,

the undoing of life

the bidding of Nometheog.

It is so."

When her tale was over, she sat staring at Galan but she did not say anything to single him out. He remembered this telling of the story. It is the same one that his mother had told him many years before. He thought about what he had seen, how the strange men had led them away. How they had killed Kaila's parents. This was the true telling, he knew, and the hunters had forgotten their own origins or twisted them to achieve something dark. It sickened him.

His mother was beside him, though he didn't recall when exactly she had arrived. It had been sometime during the story. Kaila, he noticed, was sitting close by the Mother, next to the dais. There were musicians and dancers now, but his heart did not feel warm any more. He thought of himself as a sort of abomination. This is how they viewed the hunters. That is why they wanted to kill him. He did not blame them.

XIX. Broken

Belle had hardly slept but it would be worth it for Evingh to come to his senses. She woke him from his sleep at the table; he looked directly at her, not seeing her, gripping her arm tight enough to bruise. She winced, but then took his head in her other hand. "There, now, it's just a dream, dear. Just a dream." His grip loosened and she watched as tears welled into his glassy eyes and slowly streamed down his cheeks, he cried but remained asleep. Belle reached for the vial. She was unsure if this would work, but she knew that it was her only hope to help him. She had to try it.

She gently tilted his head back. He struggled to release himself from her hold, turning his head back and forth, but she knew that she had to force him to drink it. She tightened her hold.

Gripping his head with her arm, she held his mouth open with her free hand, forcing the liquid in, and holding her hand tight over his lips. He tried to spit it out, sputters of liquid squished beneath her palm, but she held her hand firmly in place until she knew that he had swallowed it. She stepped back, watching for some sign that it had taken affect. Slowly, he blinked his eyes and stared around the room. She saw the confusion in his gaze, the failed organization of disoriented thoughts.

He looked around, trying to place where he was. He was at a table in a large kitchen. Gray and red stones made up the walls. Long, red curtains hung straight on each side of four windows on the wall opposite the hearth. Smooth, gray stones made up the floor. He tried to recall ever being here but managed only confusion. He slowly sat up straighter, looking at Belle. He took in her round face, rosy cheeks and caring expression. Had he seen her before?

"Where am I?" he asked her, holding a trembling hand up to his sweating forehead.

"You're at the king's castle," she said, calmly.

He tried to remember where he had been and recall how he had gotten here, and then the scattered fragments began to come together in his head. He remembered the beast, the nightmares, the lives that he had taken, the horrible things that he had done. With those memories came a nauseating terror. He tried to stand, to run away from this place but he fell to the floor retching.

"How did I get here?" he asked her, shaking, sobbing.

"You were brought here," she said.

He breathed deeply, covering his head with his arms, muffling his voice. "The beast brought me here," he said, remembering, but hoping he was wrong.

Belle nodded her head. "Yes," she quietly acknowledged.

Slowly, he lifted his head and met her gaze. Evingh's eyes were wide with both sorrow and anger.

He stood up, running clumsily to an exit. Belle ran after him but he did not get far out in the snow before he collapsed to his knees, wailing uncontrollably. Belle was troubled to watch anyone be so miserable. She had no words to comfort him so she put her hands on his shoulders.

"Get away from me!" He screamed at her so loudly that she heard his voice crack. He coughed and wept.

"I'll be inside if you need me," she said, knowing in her heart that he would not leave.

She went inside leaving the door open, and began cleaning his puddle of vomit off the floor. It was not the most pleasant of tasks, but she had dealt with worse. By the time she had finished, Evingh had wondered back inside and was pacing the room. He crossed his arms tightly, shaking his head.

"There's no going back," he said, more to himself than to Belle.

Belle walked closer to him, though she kept her distance. "Going back?" she asked.

He crouched onto the floor, shaking, covering his face again, "I can't undo it," he said, running his fingers through his hair in a hurried, nervous way. "I can't go back." He wrinkled his face, tears filled his eyes. His hands stopped moving and he pulled his hair, holding it in tight fists.

"Go back where?" she asked.

"I can't go back to…to when it was…all right," he said. His words were broken, full of emotion.

Belle reached her hands out to his shoulders and looked into his eyes. "Tell me," she said. "Please, tell me what you want to go back to."

He gazed at her for a moment, knowing that he should recognize her, trust her. He shook his head. "I've done terrible things. I can't undo them. I can't go back…" he shoved her away then pulled up his sleeve, staring at the brand on his skin. It was the mark of a hunter, the arrow piercing the Valka beast. "I can't undo it," he said again, rubbing his fingertips over the scar.

She walked over and looked at the mark. "This symbol has certainly been one of fear for many. When I first saw it on your arm, I thought the art was beautiful, but in a dark way, and I was terrified to look at it."

"You should be!" he said. "You should fear me, and hate me, and kill me while I'm weak."

"Well, that's not my way, dear. I am not afraid to tame a beast. I do not feel hate for anyone, and I certainly do not kill…unless I must. I am not afraid of you. Rather, I am afraid for you." She reached out for his hand. His instinct was to slap her away, but something about this woman was so tender and calming that he felt paralyzed at the moment.

"Now," she said, holding to his hand. "Let us put aside this desire to go back. It's better to move forward.

Sometimes going back is painful. So, why don't you stay here with me? Stay here and forget anything that has happened before now."

It was a long time before he spoke, he just stared at her, trying to discern why he should listen to, and trust her. He looked down at the skin brand, staring into some memory that Belle could not perceive.

"You can't imagine the things that I've done," he finally spoke.

"You're right, Evingh. Unless you tell me what has happened, I can't begin to understand." She tugged at his hand and gently led him toward the table. "Sit and eat something with me," she said.

He was reluctant, but he let her lead him to the table. He watched her intently while she brought him the last of the stew.

He looked at the stew, but shoved it away.

"I can't eat," he said.

"So, what do you feel like doing right now?" she asked.

"Being alone," he responded.

"Very well," she said. She motioned toward the door leading into the hall. "I'll not hold you here. But I'm not leaving. The kitchen is my domain."

He said no more, but turned and walked, disappearing down the hall. Belle got up to shut the outside door, through which a dry, bitter wind blew into the kitchen. She smiled as the room suddenly felt warmer. Her potion had worked.

Belle did not look for Evingh. Instead, she cleaned her kitchen, studied her cookbook, and when her eyelids grew heavy, she doused the fire and went to her small bedroom. She slid out of her bustled dress, removed her shoes and let her hair fall freely down her back. She knelt by her bedside and prayed to Saigolai. She prayed for Slatkin, for his safe return as well as the safety of the royal family and Carmina. Then she prayed for Evingh. She prayed for him to know love and for his happiness in his new life.

When she opened her eyes and pulled herself up, she did not see Evingh watching her as he leaned on the arch of the doorway. It wasn't until she was in bed, with her candle blown out, that she heard him speak.

"The things you say, when you kneel at your bedside...to whom do you speak?"

"It was a prayer to God."

"Which god?"

"The greatest of gods, Saigolai. I always pray to him."

She heard his footsteps cross the room. "Did you mean them? The things you said...about me...did you mean it?"

"Of course, dear! I would never have prayed it if I didn't."

She felt him sit beside her on the bed. "Do you think it's possible?"

"Well, why wouldn't it be?"

"I think that I already had my chance and I don't deserve another one."

I was supposed to have a mate by now," he said, "but I killed her." The words came out whispered, raspy. He closed his eyes tightly as he spoke. Belle could tell he struggled with the memories still. "I really didn't know," he said. There was a lengthy silence in the room. Belle couldn't tell if he cried or not. Many minutes passed before he spoke again. Belle was almost asleep when his voice brought her back to wakefulness. "I didn't know..." he seemed to struggle, a knot hanging in his throat, "...what I did to her." His lips quivered when he spoke. "I just wanted her. She was the one that I chose..." again there was a pause. He seemed to be locked in some memory as he spoke. "She killed herself, but it was because of what I did to her...I can't undo it. I can't go back."

Belle's eyes welled with tears as she listened to him speak.

"I wish that I could go back. I wish that I could make her understand. I didn't want to hurt her. I know that now. I've done more though. More things. I can't undo any of them and it serves me right. If I were her, I wouldn't want me. *I* don't want me. I just want it all to end." He touched the mark on his arm, feeling it in the darkness.

"And this," he said, "this brand means that I can't be unmarked. I'm a hunter. I kill things. It's what I do. I don't know another way."

Belle could tell that he was feeling desperate. He was angry at himself.

"Evingh," she said, "all humans do things that we wish we could take back. We all want to go back at some time in our lives, but you're right that we can't do that. All we can do is move forward. We must put aside our pasts and make new paths for ourselves. Otherwise you will hate yourself forever."

"I wish I could end myself, end this feeling," he said.

Belle reached out for his hand, feeling his calloused fingers in the dark. "I know dear, I know, I have feelings like that too sometimes." Evingh drew his hand away and stood up, pacing again.

"There's more than just her, though. I've done so many things. I've killed others. I killed a tavern whore and didn't even think twice about it. I killed a man and stole his horse. I've tortured men and women to get them to tell me what I needed to know. I've hung tavern wenches because my friends thought it was funny.

"But you're not that person now, Evingh. Not if you don't want to be. Seeing your wrongdoings is the first step in changing who you are."

He cut his eyes and shot her a dark glance, even though he knew she wouldn't see it in the dark. "And what would you know about changing?"

"Quite a lot, actually," she said. "The beast that you met...he used to be a man. I created the monster in him."

Evingh made a disbelieving noise, as if he thought she was trying to amuse him, as if he didn't believe her, but her tone was genuine.

"It's true," said Belle. "I'm a witch. I turned an angel into a beast. I loved him, so I kissed him. That's forbidden, to love an orostiro, to feel passion for one of Saigolai's holiest creatures. It distracts them from their calling and makes them crave mortality. I couldn't help myself, though. I kissed him! And in doing so, I doomed us both. He will always have to be a beast and I shall never know love the way that others do. Sometimes, I wish that I could go back. I wish I could undo it, but it has already past, and I still love him, even when I'm not supposed to.

So, I choose to live a loveless life, solitary. I could go out and find someone, but I don't want anyone else. I just want him." She gazed off remembering that kiss. She would never forget it. And as much as she hated herself for it, she longed for it to happen again. "You and I have more in common than you know." There were no more words between them, but Belle soon fell asleep listening to the steady rhythm of Evingh's pacing.

XX. The Ceremony

"Are you alright, my son?" Khali asked. She felt his head. "I think you need the healers to come back. You feel hot," she said, her hand on his forehead. He was tired, but he didn't feel bad the way that he had before.

"I'm okay, Mother." There was an edge of irritation to his words.

"Are you still worried about Kaila?" she asked. She reached around his shoulder and pulled him to her. "Galan, you need not worry. You are about to see. She has chosen to stay here. We will protect her."

The dancers moved closer to them and they were momentarily distracted, but then the dancers moved away.

"How did he take you?" Galan asked.

Khali just stared at her son, momentarily shocked. The expression on her face was hard to read. "Why do you ask me such a bold question?" she said, with the same irritation she had just heard in her son's voice.

"Because I want to know. I need to know! Was there ever love between you?"

Khali swallowed hard. "Yes," she whispered. "It is shameful for me to say such a thing in my homeland, but it is true."

"Do you still love him?" he asked.

"There are many kinds of love, my son. Many kinds of love."

"That did not answer my question. Do you still love him?"

"Do not make me answer that question," she pleaded.

"Please tell me," he said. "How did your pairing happen? How did he first find you?"

"Now is not the time, my son. I will tell you of it later."

"I need you to tell me before I leave," he stared into her gaze, seeking some unsaid answer in her eyes. He knew that his father was hunting him, to kill him. How he handled the situation depended entirely on his mother's story. He had pondered it while he lay between fever and awareness in the healer's hut. It had been nagging him in his mind.

His future lay in the fact. He had already decided it. There were two scenarios that acted out in his head every time he thought about the moment when he would come face to face with his father again. Either of them could happen, but the deciding factor for him would come with his mother's tale. If their love was true and deep between them, he knew that the outcome would be different than if the love was something that grew with familiarity.

Soon though, his thoughts were cast aside as his attention went to the dais. The dancers had been dancing, but it soon came to a halting stop, along with the music, and the Mother walked down the steps. Many of the stones that she wore were now aglow, and kneeling at the bottom of the dais, was Kaila. The mother reached down with stones flashing from all the gods upon her hand.

"Hear now my words, dear child," she said. "To be an Astrid, you must possess certain qualities that make you worthy of the title. The first is that you must be willing to listen to me, the Mother, for I am both wise and powerful. I have the wisdom of the gods within me, and to go against me is to defy the wisdom of the gods that shape the world.

The second quality is the desire to contribute to the tribal community. You will have a place in the tribal hut. You are too new and too young to gain a permanent place in the tribe. So, for now, I will teach you things. You will be my student. If you will allow me to be your mentor, you will gain a place among the fellow Astrids. If you can do this, then you will be well on your way to becoming an Astrid.

The third quality is that you must show respect to others, whether man, beast, or plant. For all life is worth preserving, according to Saigolai. If you feel that you have these qualities, then step forward, and I will see if the gods show that you are true to your word. Do not lie, though, for the gods can see your thoughts and they will be able to tell me if you are truthful. If you lie to me, the consequences will be unbearable. Come forth, and let the gods judge your values.

Galan leaned forward, so as to get a better look of his sister climbing the dais toward the Mother. Her blonde hair had been loosened, and it hung down her back. Her back was turned to Galan as she ascended to the platform. As she reached the Mother, the wizened woman held out a bracelet like Khali's. Many of the multicolored stones glowed in various hues and shades. A dark gray stone suddenly sparkled silver and a deep brown stone burned like a red coal, while a sandy stone shone like golden honey. The mother smiled. The pearly one she had placed as one of her teeth glowed white.

"Do you think you are capable of listening in order to learn, contributing to help others, and respecting in order to preserve life?" she asked the girl. Her voice was deep and unnerving.

Kaila looked proudly at the Mother. "Yes," she said. "I am capable of them all," she said, proudly.

The stones shone more brightly and the Mother nodded her head as she placed the bracelet carefully on the girl's arm, then she turned to the tribe. "Let us welcome Kaila to our tribe. She will serve me as a Hungawki in the Mundara hut."

Kaila turned to look at the new tribe, and she was suddenly being showered with gifts and the women were again dancing and singing loudly.

Galan shook his head, then turned to his Mother. "If I didn't know any better, I'd think that they drugged her to say that. All life has value? Do they all abide by that?"

His mother nodded her head.

Galan wrinkled his brow and frowned. "Then why were they so ready to kill me earlier?"

Khali sighed heavily. "We do appreciate all life and we wish to preserve it. But you must understand that by now, there are other tribes, such as the hunters, who wish to slay us, rape us, or carry us away into slavery. We value life, but we must be willing to preserve our own lives when faced with such a choice. These women are afraid, Galan, and they have good reason to be."

"Can't there be another way?" he asked.

She shook her head. "Not until the fear is replaced with trust. If you were these women, would you trust the strangers that you saw?"

Galan didn't say anything, he just looked over at Kaila, who was now having her hair blackened and slicked back like the other women.

"I don't trust a lot of things," he said.

XXI. A Kind of Love

Galan awoke early in the day, tired from the late night, but ready to continue. He did not want to leave his mother and sister, but he knew that it was his only choice. The angel would take care of him, he knew, but he was more concerned with how the tribe would fare once the angel left them alone. He was packing a supply sack when his mother came into the room.

"Are you ready yet?" she asked him.

"No," he replied frankly. "Why can't I just stay here with you and Kaila?" he asked.

"Galan, I know that we will miss each other, but finding your destiny may prove to be more important than just me or you or your sister. You may have the ability to do great things."

He looked at his mother, nodding. "You know what my gift is, don't you?"

She nodded. "I suspect that I do, but I cannot be sure."

"It's the same as yours," he said.

She shrugged. "I do not know that, and neither does anyone else. Your gift may be the same as mine, but it can also be quite different. Sometimes they are different when they go to the men."

"Mother, I am about to leave. I'll be all the way on the other side of the island. It's time you tell me the truth. I want to know about your gift. I want to know about you and my father. I want to know about your pairing and how he stole your gift."

She nodded. "Now is the best time to hear it," she agreed. "If there is ever such a time for these things," she said.

She sat down on the bed, staring at the floor and inhaled deeply. "The first time that I laid eyes on your father, he was wounded. I knew that his leg was broken. I also knew that he was a hunter. I was cautious, but I knew that the right thing to do was to help him. What kind of a person would I be to let him lie there?

I tended to his wounds, and set his broken leg. I brought him food and water and looked after him until he was well enough to be on his own. It was many days that I looked after him. I only knew some of the words in his language, and he did not know any in mine. Before I left, I knew that he was fond of me. I don't think that, as a hunter, he knew how to thank me. He pulled me to him and kissed me. I pushed him away and struck him. I was already promised to another.

I was paired by the time I ever saw your father again. There was a Ward. His name was Numal. Numal was a Shaman, and he chose me because of my spirit-gift. I chose him because I knew that he would make me a leader of the Astrids. At the time, I wanted it more than anything else.

Shamans are powerful, and like me, he could speak to the gods. That was my gift, son. I could speak to the gods. I did not need the stones like the Mother. I could simply summon the one that I wished to speak to and speak to them. I could ask them for favors, I could challenge them. My power was often too much for me to control, but I knew that a Shaman, like Numal, could help me understand what I could do.

One day, Numal was not with me, he had already left to go back across the island, I was fishing with some of my sisters. I heard the hunters coming. I was told they were coming. I did everything that I could to get the other women to safety. I knew that they would come, but in that moment, I thought that I could fight them. I thought that the gods would come to my aid, but they didn't. They were favoring the hunters. I knew, as soon as I saw your father, who he was. I knew that he was the one I had healed.

He returned my gift of life by taking me. I was blindfolded, but I could hear. I knew that he had killed another for me. Then at the first chance, he branded his mark to me." She pointed to her chest, to the black symbol, a circle with a bird inside. The hunters called it the caged bird of life. Galan had seen the brand so often that it was just another part of his mother, like her eyes, her hair, her voice. It was just part of her. Being so young, he had never considered that it was forced onto her. "At first I was angry, pained, grieving. I did not understand why he had taken me. I saved his life and he stole me away from everyone that I loved. But the gods spoke to me. I knew that I would give birth to you. After that, I knew that there was no going back. You see, once an Astrid has been stolen, they are tainted to the tribe. I knew that I could not go home. After some weeks, the gods became silent to me.

213

I could no longer hear them. I realized that Volkhan had taken my gift. I had been told that it could happen, but I never believed that it would happen to me. I tried to escape many times, but it never ended well for me. There's a reason that Volkhan is such a mighty hunter. He always tracked me down.

I could read his emotions, though. It hurt him that I wanted to leave. He believed that I should be devoted to him. I should feel honor at serving him. After all, in a way, I was exactly what I thought I would be. I had married the leader of the tribe. This was the one thought that brought me comfort before you were born.

But then you came, and I knew that you were my life. You would have to be taught to be a good man, especially knowing the things that your father would no doubt teach you." A tear slipped from Khali's soft brown eye but she smiled. "You ask me if there was love," she said. "The answer is yes, you are our love, without him, I could not have you, and although he is cruel sometimes, I know that he doesn't know another way to be. Can you blame a wolf for killing a rabbit? It is his nature to be this way, and if he were any other way, he would not be the leader of the hunters."

"And now I'm home and I could not be more proud of you, my son, no matter the outcome of our present situation, please understand that I am proud of you. You warm my heart. To think that you saved Kaila, and me, it makes me happy."

Galan was having a hard time taking in what she was telling him. It made his thoughts toward his father more complicated. The fact that his mother loved him, despite the things he had done to her pained him. She was in the same situation as him. If Volkhan came, neither of them would be able to defeat him. They were weak.

XXII. Goodbyes

Slatkin opened his eyes, feeling rest, peace that he had not felt for many years. The Mother was standing over him, a glowing grin spread across her face.

"Did you enjoy your dreams?" she asked.

Slatkin sat up slowly, remembering suddenly where he was, alarmed that he had let himself sleep for so long without remembering his quest.

"The boy," he said.

The Mother cackled. "They are all safe, including the boy. He is healing much faster than you. Although I think that one of our healers has taken a special interest in him…perhaps he'll return for the Lauming when they are both older."

Slatkin then felt of his chest, where the blade had pierced his heart earlier. There was no sign of pain or even a scar. "My father," he said, "he kept the flower, didn't he?"

The Mother's eyebrows lifted. "I told you before I started the treatment that it was required for your healing. I used it, as I should. One as powerful as you has no need for it."

Slatkin nodded. "I owe you something for your healing," he said.

The Mother shrugged. "You gave me a new daughter. She is valuable in many ways. For one such as I, there is no greater gift. I wish for my tribe to flourish. Without the wishes of the gods speaking in my mind, I'm still sure that keeping them safe is my greatest desire."

"I will give you the blessings of my father," he said. "That was already agreed upon, but there must be something more that I could do. You did not have to heal me, only the mortals."

"I healed you, not out of your wishes, but out of your father's. Saigolai is forgiving, but he also has much to do, and he needs you to do it."

"Again, I give you my thanks," he said.

Slatkin stepped into the healer's hut where Galan had been healed. His mother and sister were there with his healers. His mother smiled as she held him to her chest, silent tears slid down her face.

"My son," she said. "Do not be afraid, I know that the gods are with you!" She took an amulet from around her neck and placed it on his. "I am not a huntress, but this amulet is believed by the hunters to bring good luck. It may, or it may not, but son, I want you to keep it. Not as a memory of the hunters, but as a memory of me. I will see you at the Lauming, but it will be a long time until then." He could smell the oils that she used on her skin on the amulet. It was a woody, musky, sweet smell.

"I'll think of you every day," he said. She returned his words with a bittersweet smile. "And I will think of you as well, my son, with great pride in my heart."

Kaila embraced him next. "Thank you again for saving my life," she whispered. Galan couldn't help his smile.

He looked around the hut. "Are you sure that you want to stay here, Kaila?"

She smiled. "Yes," she said. "I told you before that you must leave to gain your power, but mine is here, I know it. They will take care of me and teach me things that are good."

Galan nodded. "As long as I know that's what *you* really want."

She nodded her head. "I want it, I promise."

She grabbed his hand and put a stone there. It was a grey stone speckled with black and silver. "This is Khanhine's stone. Keep it. I have another one."

He nodded. "I'll keep it," he promised.

He looked at Slatkin then, breathing deeply.

"It is time," said Slatkin.

He nodded and started to leave, but an arm stopped him. The healer, the young, quiet one that had painted his face stared at him, her eyes piercing through him. She held something against his chest. He pulled his gaze from her eyes and looked down at the feathers she held there, large, sleek and black, the feathers of the kraelvins.

He looked at them, confused and slowly lifted his hands to them, then looked into her eyes. She still stared at him with the piercing gaze that made him feel uneasy.

"What's this for?" he asked.

"Take them, son," said his mother.

The healer nodded her head and walked away, satisfied that he had taken her gift.

He looked at Slatkin, who smiled knowingly. "Keep them safe," he said. "I told you that kraelvins are special, not like other birds." Galan tucked them into the pouch at his side with the stone from his sister and they turned to leave. The Mother waited at the bridge on the edge of Astrid territory.

"Thank you," Galan said to her, "for not killing me."

She cackled loudly. "I would have killed you," she admitted. "Thank you for teaching me the things that I had forgotten," she said. She motioned for one of the guards at the bridge, and then to Galan. The guard held a bow and a case of arrows out to him. "Let these arrows defend me and my children for many generations and keep you safe so that you will return to our family."

Galan reached out for them, astonished at her act of kindness.

"Why would you give me this?"

The Mother puffed on the kial twig in her mouth, "because I want to see you again, some day."

Galan nodded in understanding. "I will be back, then," he said as he positioned the quiver of arrows across his back.

Slatkin began walking. The old man and the boy crossed the bridge and Galan suddenly felt like it was too long until the Lauming.

XXIII. Father and Son

Galan was quiet after they left. Slatkin didn't have to say anything to him. He knew the fear and anticipation the boy felt. He could see it in the colors that swirled through his soul.

They walked on through the morning, carefully stepping through the snow-covered roots on the forest floor. The morning was cold, but the sky was overcast. They traveled all morning without passing words between them unless it was necessary. Eventually the necessity was there. Far in the distance, Slatkin could hear them. The hunters. They had found a way around the river and they were gaining speed. He stopped, attuning his senses to the direction of the noise. Galan stopped and turned to him when he realized that the Orostiro was not moving.

"What's wrong?" Galan asked.

Slatkin sighed. "We'll eat lunch and press on," he said.

Somewhere in the distance, a wolf howled.

"Did you hear that?" whispered Galan, stringing an arrow in his bow. "A wolf!"

"You should not see it as an enemy," said Slatkin. "Do not be too quick with your weapon."

"But the wolves will devour us!" he exclaimed. "I've seen what they can do. Wolves are never a good omen for a hunter."

Slatkin looked at him for a moment. Then smiled. "It is good that you are not a hunter," he reminded him.

Galan pondered what he said as he stared down at the bow and arrow. Then he nodded his head with understanding and stowed the arrow in his quiver.

They then unpacked briefly to eat. Slatkin did not press conversation, but attuned his senses to what he could hear in the distance. The hunters were traveling very fast. It was no doubt part of the Shadow's hold on them. He heard the wolves also. Their sound was coming from the West. The hunters were south of them.

After Galan had eaten, he sat back and looked very soberly at Slatkin. "What if the Wards do not take me in? What will happen to me?"

"I will never abandon you. I'll take you back to the king. He will be glad to have you at the castle."

"So why don't I just go there now? If you know that I'll be safe there and you know that he will accept me?"

Slatkin sighed. "Things like this are never so easy," he said. Just then the howling of wolves pierced the air. Galan reached for his bow again, but Slatkin motioned with his arm for Galan to stop the action.

"I tell you again, they are not the enemy. Put your weapon away and we will pack up and leave." There was a sting of urgency in Slatkin's voice that made Galan obey without thinking twice. Soon they were on their way again, moving much quicker than before. Another howl pierced the air, different in frequency, a different wolf...then another howl. Much louder and higher pitched than the others. This was no wolf. It was a creature of darkness. Slatkin looked at Galan, deep pains erupted in his bones...how could he explain to the boy that neither of them was prepared for what was about to happen?

"Galan, I need to you to find a safe place. There are more than wolves surrounding us. I need you to hide."

The orostiro knew that Galan understood far more than Slatkin wanted him to. He could see it in the colors of the boy's soul.

"It's him, isn't it?" Galan asked, his eyes wide with terror, the color draining from his face.

Slatkin could only nod. "And there's another," he warned. "You've seen what they can do, and I'm telling you that you must hide!" Slatkin looked into the boy's eyes. Galan nodded and ran to find the best place to hide. Slatkin did not try to hide, but he felt the pains in his hands accelerate. Slowly, it traced through him. He had enough time to shed the outer fur coat and take off his boots before he was too impaired to move.

His transformation began, tracing its way through his bones and muscles. He felt every stretch, every tear, every expansion as his bones grew into long claws, the face of a wolf, and large leathery wings. Soon he was standing twelve feet in height, the image of a wolfish creature with large, black, leathery wings. The weakness and previous pains melted away into power. It was a power that he would use to save Galan.

The wolves and the creatures were howling fiercely now, getting closer, gaining speed. The two unnatural creatures seemed to have some dizzying screech following their howls. Slatkin waited patiently for his prey.

They were upon him all too soon. The wolves, he knew were here to help him. And he knew right away which ones were of the Shadow. Volkhan came running on two legs. Half dead, scarred skin and half mechanical wolf-demon, he ran straight for Slatkin, almost equaling him in size.

The orostiro stood his ground, and the two threw blows at each other. Slatkin raked his claws across the metal and skin of the Shadow creature he faced. Volkhan merely laughed a growling taunt, then kneed Slatkin in the gut, knocking him to the ground, they struggled, a mass of leathery wings, fur, flesh, and metal. Slatkin rolled and stood again, shaking and unfurling his wings. One of the nearby wolves ran, grabbing Volkhan's arm in their vice-like grip, shaking its head and growling. Volkhan let out a yelp and then pummeled the wolf in the face. Blood and fur flew through the air as the two wolf creatures let out two very different, yet ear piercing sounds. Slatkin lunged at the Shadow-wolf, knocking him back.

He tried to get a grip on the hunter's face to see his eyes, he needed to see his eyes for his power to work, but Volkhan's head was violently shaking back and forth as he let out unnatural guttural growls. Slatkin felt the cold metal claws ripping flesh along his ribs, and he let out a roar of pain. He pulled himself away and rolled through the snow. Volkhan stood, laughing. "You are no match for the strength of the Shadow!"

Slatkin reached out, aware of the pig grunts and squeals mingled with howls and growls of the wolves around them, but they had chosen their own fight, and he could not help them. Galan was his only task at the moment. The shadow wolf howled and lunged at him again. Slatkin dodged and grabbed the hunter's leg, knocking him off balance. Another wolf threw itself at him, keeping him in the snow. Slatkin regained his footing and reached out, gaining an advantage. He grabbed the hunter's torso. He flung him and he flew through the air, snapping tree limbs before he landed on his side. A steamy fog started rising through the forest as the heat from the trees hit the cold air. Volkhan stood again, laughing.

Galan watched from a ledge nearby. He saw the wolves and Slatkin. Then he saw the other two creatures. They looked nothing like the men he knew them as before, but he was certain that it was Haz and his father. There was no doubt. He could feel it. He watched as they struggled. He nocked an arrow and aimed at the creature that had been his father, but he was frozen in terror, torn between running to help, staying hidden, or just walking out and surrendering himself. He knew that he could probably not fight the beast, for if Slatkin was struggling, he knew that he would be dead already. But he also understood that if he stayed hidden, they would find him eventually. He saw no way for the outcome to be in Slatkin's favor. As Volkhan slammed through rock-hard branch after branch of the kial thierens and ignited their flames, he realized the indestructible force that his father had become. He knew he had to help Slatkin, no matter the cost. He began the descent from the ledge. He carefully found footholds, forcing himself down. But as he turned around at the bottom of the ledge, he was stilled with fear.

The other creature was there. Something resembling man, boar, and machine stood waiting for him. A squeal of terrible delight, fueled by the Shadow, erupted from the creature as it threw up its arms and bared huge tusks. He advanced quickly on the boy, charging quickly. Galan ducked and rolled sideways as the boar slammed into the icy, rock wall of the mountain. It shook off the effect, glanced at Galan, then turned to the wolf attack, which had become more violent. He made a split decision and charged the group of wolves instead. Galan took a moment to catch his breath, not realizing that he had been holding it.

"You tried that one before," Volkhan roared at the angel, holding out his arms, "but I'm not so easy to kill!" As he spoke, there erupted a hissing sound from the injured trees. Galan looked towards the branches to see their broken limbs turning red and flaming. In that moment, the Shadow-wolf charged at the Orostiro. Another wolf ran at Volkhan, knocking him sideways. Slatkin threw himself at the creature and he fell to the ground. Slatkin pinned him down and grabbed his head as the wolves struggled to grip his limbs. The orostiro looked into the dark creature's eyes, there was humanity still there. Not much, but it was there. A loud low, unnatural growl was erupting from the Shadow-wolf as it forcefully shook its head back and forth to rid itself of the imposing grip of the angel.

Then he stopped, subdued as the angel caught Volkhan's gaze, and locked into his soul with his eyes. But before he could speak to the humanity left in the creature, Haz appeared, charging the group on the ground. The wolves could not hold the hunter down any longer. They dispersed in barks and matted fur as the boar charged through them. Slatkin held the hunter tightly but lost his grip as the wolves were thrown aside and the boar slammed into him. He rushed to get up, but Volkhan, seeing opportunity, leapt at the orostiro and reached out with his jaws, biting into Slatkin's throat. The pain was intense, unbearable, as flesh was ripped from his throat by the Shadow-creature's teeth. He knew then that he could not win the fight. His throat had been ripped from his body. He saw the boy, but without speech, he could not instruct him. His breath was painfully leaving his body with his throat. How Saigolai would save him this time, he did not know. He forced himself up, blood streaming down the front of him and puddling in the snow but perhaps he had a last effort in him. He rushed the Shadow-wolf, knocking him down again, but then the Shadow-boar pounded into him and his breath was too far gone to move again.

Galan found his footing as he ran to help the wolves but as he approached, he watched as the creature that used to be his father ripped the throat from the other. Slatkin staggered back in shock and fell over in the snow, but then he got up again and Galan heard himself screaming in anger at his father's actions as he saw the blood and mangled mess that Slatkin now was. There was a moment of hope as Slatkin charged his father, but then Haz intervened and Galan ran closer to them, preparing for what he must do. The wolves slowly backed away, their tails hanging low, their ears pointed back, as they growled with rage and fear. His father gained his feet, and ground the angel's flesh in his metal teeth, then spit the gore onto the snow. It spattered into a mess of red and grey fur.

Then he laughed, showing blood stained teeth. It was a triumphant, evil laugh. A cold voice spoke, not the one his father had used before, but another one, a voice that spoke from the depths of the void.

"Saigolai, you fool! There is no life you make that I cannot take away!" He let out another high-pitched laugh and then Volkhan noticed his son. Galan knew that he could not fight him, but perhaps he could reason with the part of his father that remained, for the way that the hunter beheld his son at this moment carried an expression of the old Volkhan.

"Galan, you're safe," he said, walking forward, struggling to keep his voice genuine.

Galan just nodded, he had an arrow strung into his bow, and his stare was set at his father's eyes.

"That's my boy," he said, his voice sending chills down Galan's spine, it terrified him to stare at this beast that was not his father, yet carried such a similar likeness, from his voice to his mannerisms.

He heard the boar creature stepping up behind him.

"Son," Volkhan spoke, "come with me and I'll see that you are strong like me. Come see what I've done. Look how easily I took down that beast that captured you," he boasted. Galan was slightly sickened at the sight of the orostiro's blood dripping from his father's teeth, sliding down his metal chin.

Galan thought for a moment that he would play along, but realized that he couldn't, as he walked over and glanced down at Slatkin. Anger surged in him. He looked calmly at his father. "Is that what you think happened?" he asked.

Volkhan's eyes narrowed. It took a moment to respond, as Volkhan fought some un-named emotion inside him.

"What are you implying, boy?" he asked. His own voice was back, "You went with him willingly?" He growled, giving voice to what he had already reasoned, but did not want to believe. Galan could see the hurt in his father's eyes. Everything about the fierceness in this creature's face, blended with the realization of betrayal in his father's expression, sent shivers down his spine. He would have run away if he could have. His hands shook so hard that it was difficult to keep hold to his bow, but his thoughts were now of Kaila and his mother. He could not let his father find them. The creature walked quickly forward, Galan released an arrow, but the creature only flinched as it ripped into his chest. He was suddenly upon him, grabbing Galan's face in his hands. The grip was tight. Immediate, piercing pain jabbed into his skull. The creature pulled him close.

"Where are your mother and the girl?" it asked, he was released with a shove into the snow. "Their trail went cold at the river."

It took a moment for Galan to collect himself. Suddenly, he felt braver at the mention of his mother and sister. He stood up taller, prouder.

"If I tell you, you'll kill them."

His father shook his head. "Not necessarily. I have my reasons for keeping them alive."

"I would never tell you even if I did know! I would rather you kill me now, rip out my throat and leave it for the wolves, like you did the beast!" he said, motioning at Slatkin.

There was a guttural grunt behind him as the other beast started to advance, but Volkhan raised his arm for the other creature to stop.

"Son," he said, stepping forward. "Why do you always go against my wishes?" He looked sincerely down at Galan and suddenly, he looked more like the old hunter Volkhan than the wolf-monstrosity that he had become.

Galan stared at his father, deep into his eyes. "Because I have my own wishes and I'm a better man than you!" He did not hesitate in speaking. The things that he had always wanted to say to his father slipped easily from his tongue.

Suddenly, there was a cackling, high-pitched laugh that came from deep within the creature. Haz grabbed him from behind with a terrifying squeal. Then the Shadow-wolf looked at Galan, the hunter was now gone and a shadow-creature stared back, no trace of his father could be seen.

"Man?" it asked, reaching out to the boy with sharp, metal claws. "I am no longer a man! I have become more than man has ever desired." The hunter's claws dug into Galan's shoulder, both in the front and the back. Paralyzing agony spread throughout his arms and back, down to his ribs. Galan, though hardly able to breathe through the pain, gritted his teeth and stared into the creature's eyes.

"You only know the desires of twisted men!"
Galan said, gritting his teeth through the pain, he felt his
eyes rolling back in his head. His voice had left him, but
he forced words through the pain. "Your real dream is to
know my desires, but you never will! My desires are too
pure for someone as tainted as you to comprehend." It was
a whisper. The shadow-wolf howled in fury and suddenly,
Galan felt it. He knew then what his spirit gift felt like. He
was powerful, like the Mother, but more so. He was
speaking directly to Nomethoeg. To the dark god! It was
something that would make a normal human's mind turn
dark and insane. Yet, he was sure that his mind was still
his own, and that the god could not manipulate his
thoughts. In fact, he was sure that his own thoughts were
hidden from the god because he chose it to be so. And,
unlike the Mother, he didn't need to use a stone.

"Nometheog," he said, "you have stolen my father,
but you will not steal me!" he shouted. "Khanhine will
help me!" Suddenly, the boar released his hold, and there
was a fit of howls and grunting squeals. Galan reached for
his hunting knife as Volkhan released him. The boy
shouted to the gods who opposed Nometheog for aid and

suddenly, the kial tree above them dripped viscous, hot flame from its broken boughs. As it did, it landed on the hunter's neck, just before Galan leapt up and dug in the blade of the dagger, slicing the creature's throat with both fire and metal. The fire made slicing through the metal neck easy, but then the blade became too hot to hold. Flames had ignited and were tracing their way up the blade. He stared down with wide eyes, realizing what he had just done, as both he and the creature fell into the snow. He released the handle, as flames ignited from within his father's body and spread to his own hands. Then he turned to the boar creature, but the wolves had already ripped the remaining flesh from the shell of metal and wires that was left of the body. Galan just stared in shock at the scene around him, feeling queasy and outside of himself.

Slatkin lay in a familiar place. He was beyond life, but before death, drifting in the realm of angels. He couldn't speak, he couldn't breathe, yet death could not come for the immortals. He dreamed and listened and watched what he could. His father was there, instructing him, but his words seemed far away. He saw Galan confronting his father, but the beast was not yet striking him. He saw Saigolai and there were two other gods. Khanhine and Thiera, goddess of fire. They stood with hands interlocked and a warm sun seemed to spread from around them over the scene and soon Slatkin could see nothing but a hot, orange glow.

Then, it seemed like millennia later, yet somehow earlier, when he was much younger, he lay on the grass. It was a warm, summer night. It was all he could do not to stare at the witch beside him. The colors of her soul spread out far around her. The trees around her seemed to change from black to honey colored. The grass seemed to hum with life and even the little bugs that crawled around seemed to pulsate with glowing life. Her hair burned fiery red, like a blaze of life filling his soul. He concentrated on the stars, stealing glances at her when he felt that he could.

When she looked at him, when his eyes met hers, he saw colors there that he had never seen before: new colors, new things, beautiful things. He reached out to touch the fire of her hair, to test its reality. It warmed his cold hands and her hands traced over his skin, igniting a flame throughout his limbs. Then she touched her lips to his and suddenly he could see things he never could before. He could name the new colors and feel the new things. The glow she emanated pierced through him and there was nothing then that mattered except her. He pulled her closer, wrapping himself in her embrace. Her lips moved to his neck and he felt then that something was wrong. He pushed her away and all the colors and shapes faded away with her. Everything faded, the darkness, the shapes, the hues, the matter.

He was now in a place away from time, weight or matter. All was white and cloudy around him.

Then his father, Saigolai, sat beside him.

"Father," he said. He looked around, but saw no trace of his Belle, or the trees, or the stars. It was only father and son, in a world of blank white.

"Son," his father said.

"Where did she go?"

"Don't worry about her, she's safe."

Slatkin tried to recall how he came to be here, but how does anyone get to a place out of time, out of life?

"Where was I?" he asked, trying to reason, to remember.

"Exactly where you were supposed to be, doing what you were supposed to, my son," he said, then Saigolai smiled at his son. "Nometheog thinks that he has conquered you. That is to my advantage."

Slatkin remembered then with a great disappointment. "Galan!" he whispered.

Saigolai nodded. "He's much better off than you are at the moment!" Saigolai laughed. "Son, I know that you have made mistakes, but do not think that you have failed. The world is, indeed, changing. You have earned the chance to dream. You have given the boy to the gods of life. We owe you some reward before we send you on to your next task. Now, I'll leave you where you want to be. After all, it will be a long time before your body will regain its life...a long time before you can behold her with your human eyes.

Saigolai started to walk away, but turned back to him. "A gift," he said, and then he released the pink flower that the Mother had needed for the ceremony. It was full and renewed. It slowly twirled through the space between father and son. Slatkin reached out to grab it and his father faded away. He looked at the flower and soon, the flower was fading into dreams. Dreams of love and bliss and beautiful life, dreams of Belle.

Miles and times away, Belle was having the same dreams of Slatkin.

XXIV. Numb

Galan stared around at the carnage, in awe, then down to his father. He held his breath, tears streamed from his eyes, though he could not feel them, as he realized what he had just done. Despite the fear of Volkhan, Galan also felt the loss. The fire still steamed and sizzled from inside of the hunter's transformed body, more lava dripped from the trees, landing on his father's body, melting the metal, and burning the flesh. It felt to him like more than he could endure. He looked over at Slatkin's mutilated throat, at the blood and gore scattered over the snow and he felt weakened, nauseous, and numb.

He inhaled a deep breath. He heard soft footsteps approaching from behind him. He turned to see that the wolves were now men and women. Many of them he remembered having seen at the tavern. He knew that he had been taught to fear them. They were the Khanhine-Lupah. He was not afraid. They had saved him because he had called upon Khanhine.

He was too overwhelmed to speak. Saltook, owner of the Howling Wolf tavern, an aged man, approached him and laid a gentle hand on his shoulder.   "You did the right thing, son," he said. "I know it's hard, but you didn't have any other choice."

"He was my father!" Galan exclaimed.

Saltook patted his back.   "He used to be your father." His voice was very sobering. "The thing you just killed now, that's not a man. That's a creature of Shadow. Your father was killed by *that* thing, not you. If anything, you've set your father free from its hold.

"I don't know what to do," he admitted with a quivering voice. It was true. There was no way to express what he was currently feeling.   He didn't feel the motivation to do anything. He didn't care about his gift, even after feeling it so strongly moments before. He didn't feel like traveling to the Wards to learn to use it. He just wanted to go back to his mother and his sister and bring his father and the old man back.

Saltook nodded, "I understand, son, but see here, we didn't come to help you for nothing. You must go on with the task. We'll accompany you to the land of the Wards, your kinsmen. It was important to your friend to get you there, and he was important to us."

Galan expressed confusion. "But how did you know where we were traveling?" he asked.

"Your friends, the Scithronians. They've got a seer, and she saw that this would happen. We were asked to come help you. We've been following you since you left the Astrid lands."

"But why? Why is it that important for me to go there?" Galan asked.

"The seer knows of your gift. You can speak to the gods as if you are one of them, though you are mortal. You are hunted by more gods than Nometheog. Some of them wish to protect you, others wish to kill you, and even more of them, such as Nometheog, wish to do worse than kill you. We are here to protect you. For Khanhine and for Saigolai.

"I don't think I can go," said Galan. He sat down in the snow, feeling weary. He reached a hand out to his father's face, feeling the coldness of his father's dead skin. There was alarm when he noticed his own burnt and bleeding hands. One of the others walked over and began wrapping pieces of cloth around his palms. "I can't go right now," he said. "It just seems...wrong...to just leave them here."

"Should we bury them?" asked Saltook.

Galan shrugged his shoulders. It was a long time before he finally turned to the others with a silent nod. Before their very eyes, the men and women appeared as wolves again. They began to sniff the ground and then took to digging graves in the snow. Galan sat numbly staring before him as the wolves worked, digging two graves. His father's remains were buried in the first, and the remains of the boar creature, Haz, were laid to rest in the second.

"What about the old man?" he asked.

Saltook smiled, knowingly. "I think Saigolai wants that one to stay put."

"We should at least cover him then," said Galan.

Saltook nodded. "Yes, I'm sure that's a good idea." He nodded to the wolves, which began pawing in the snow, slowly covering Slatkin's body. Galan sat staring at his father's grave for a long time. Eventually, the shadows in the trees grew long, the coldness of the evening settled in, and he was aware that he had to keep moving. Now he wanted to go back, to talk to Kaila. He knew now something of what she had felt. His feelings twisted and knotted inside his gut, and every breath seemed a pain for him. The wolves did not transform back to human shapes, except for Saltook, who sat close by, smoking a kial twig.

After many hours, he moved closer to Galan. "Do you want to say something?"

Galan shook his head. Even if he had something to say, he was sure that the words would not escape. Many minutes passed in stillness and shock. Saltook finally patted him on the back to reassure him.

"We need to leave. This place is not safe any longer. If you do not want to travel to the Wards, at least let us go back to the tavern. We'll take care of you there, and there will be a warm bed and good food."

Galan finally nodded and walked forward with the wolves. He traveled forward, numb and lost. He wondered so many things then, about how things could have been different, but he knew that there was no way to change the things that had taken place. No matter how he had worked it out in his mind, there was ultimately nothing that he could have done to save his father. Eventually, Kaila would have killed him, or he would have ended in some other way, but it did not stop the horrific feeling of guilt and loss that he could not undo. Galan did not notice where the wolves led him, he walked forward, following. Numb.

XXV. Salvaging

Xandra's black boots crunched through the icy sludge surrounding the fallen mahldrusecs. Her mission here was to recover lost parts. She knew that she was in the right spot, but even though her eye scanned every detail in the area, she saw no bodies, and there were not heat signatures to signify life. There were two mounds of dirt, but nothing more. She scanned the area with her cybernetic eye, recording a video of the scene around her for Shekley. Logic told her that they were possibly beneath the dirt. She held her hand above one of the mounds, sensing with electromagnetic pulses, what lay beneath the dirt. There was a strong pull beneath her palms. She knew then that the bodies were there, beneath the ground, waiting for her to salvage them.

She spoke to report the news to Shekley. "I have found them. They are buried beneath the ground."

"Well, dig them up!" The voice that responded was the cold, raspy, impatient one that she didn't want to hear, the voice that controlled her when she wanted to get away.

She did as she was told. She did not have a tool for digging. She possessed no tools, only weapons. She had been built as a killer. She leaned down pushing the snow and dark earth away, digging with her metaloid hands until she began to reach metal and flesh beneath the shallow graves. Two of her kind lay, slain by some force that Shekley had yet to understand. She dug until she pulled the first one free. Volkhan, that had been his name, and so it would be again, if Shekley felt that he was worthy. She dug into the second grave until again, she reached metal and flesh. There were more parts than body. Haz lay in pieces. She stacked the parts neatly in a pile so as to be easier to carry. When she was sure that she had gotten them all, she laid the parts of Haz on top of Volkhan, ripped the rope from the waist belt of Volkhan's stagnant body, tied the pieces so that they would stay in place and started the long trek back to the barren lands, leaving a trail in the snow as she pulled the bodies behind her.

Gods of Sark

Saigolai g	od of life
Sari g	oddess of Healing
Nometheog	god of void (dark god)
Vishka	goddess of suffering (dark goddess)
Selfirin	Creation/greater light
Luna	Order/lesser light
Kialo	Earth elements/nature
Kristiniva	Weather
Adrianna	Ocean/water
Dracinus	Ice and preservation
Thiera	Fire
Khanhine	Hunting
Hawitha	Gathering and harvesting
Madrig	weaving and artistry
Svengha	Navigation/travel
Khilak	Chaos (dark god)/twin to Khilis
Khilis	Deception (dark goddess) /twin to Khilak
Amicus	Messenger
Tahlain	Time

Orostiri

Slatkin   Retribution (almost banished, saved from the void by Belle)

Nuvil   Truth (banished to void, Truth became lies, deceived by Khilis)

Tintul   Wisdom

Shival   Honor (banished to void, honor became greed and ambition, gave in to temptations of Khilak in wartime.)

Morahail   Hope (banished to void after losing that which was his to wield to Nometheog's reasoning)

Slumil   Redemption (was banished and brought back with the help of Tintul.)

Vetha   Freedom (banished to void for being too war-like. Gave in to Vishka's ways)

I would like to thank Cindi West for being my pre-reader, my husband for being so patient as my personal technology teacher, and my daughters who fill my life with joy.

I dedicate this book to my mother, Elna Faye Barbour Stewart. May the afterlife be better to you than life on Earth!
I am finally understanding the lessons you taught me.
Thank you.

www.ingramcontent.com/pod-product-compliance
Lightning Source LLC
Chambersburg PA
CBHW071143170626
46809CB00002B/744